THE DUKE'S PROPOSAL

Miss Lydia Richmond has no wish for a husband; indeed, she and her best friend, Lady Alice, are determined to enjoy the company of the cavalry officers who have recently arrived in the vicinity. However, when circumstances prompt the Duke of Stenning to propose, Lydia knows it would be foolish to refuse. After all, he is in his prime — handsome enough, and quite possibly the most eligible bachelor in the kingdom. But will a marriage without love lead to heartbreak?

FENELLA J. MILLER

THE DUKE'S PROPOSAL

Complete and Unabridged

LINFORD
Leicester

First published in Great Britain in 2013

First Linford Edition
published 2014

A catalogue record for this book is available
from the British Library.

ISBN 978–1–4448–2118–5

Published by
F. A. Thorpe (Publishing)
Anstey, Leicestershire

Set by Words & Graphics Ltd.
Anstey, Leicestershire
Printed and bound in Great Britain by
T. J. International Ltd., Padstow, Cornwall

This book is printed on acid-free paper

1

'Mama, it is more than a year since Papa passed away. I believe we could attend the assembly at Stenning without causing a scandal.' Lydia reached out and squeezed her mother's hand. 'A ball is exactly what we both need before the arrival of Uncle Edward next week. I wish he was not coming, for I am not overly fond of him.'

Her mother smiled. 'My love, my brother-in-law is a perfectly pleasant gentleman; I cannot think why you have taken him in such dislike. He cannot be blamed for inheriting the title from Father and, as far as I'm aware, he has no intention of interfering with our lives in any way. Ravenscroft remains mine for my lifetime, as does the interest from the trust fund and the income from the estate. Also, your inheritance is substantial, and kept quite separate

1

from the estate funds.'

'I know that, Mama, so why does he wish to come here at all? He came to the funeral; surely that's enough? Papa and he were not close, were they?'

Her mother fiddled with the buttons on her sleeve before answering. 'They had a falling-out many years ago, before you were born. I expect he wishes he had made his peace with his brother before your papa was taken ill.'

Lydia jumped up, shook out the creases from her morning gown, and prepared to depart. 'In which case I shall say no more about it, and make an effort to welcome him as the future owner of my home and the head of the household.' Her mother was obviously ready to forgive and forget, so she must do the same.

'Have we purchased tickets for the assembly, my dear? I do hope it is not already oversubscribed — I can see you have quite set your heart on going.'

'I sent Jenny into town two days ago. All we have to decide is what we are going to wear. It seems an age since either of us was wearing anything but black and lavender.'

'We are fortunate, my love, that gowns still have a high waist.' She laughed. 'Imagine having to wear a ball gown that was outmoded!'

'You could not be out of fashion if you tried, Mama. You look more like my sister than my parent. Indeed, your hair is as golden as it always was and I swear you have hardly any more wrinkles than I.'

'Despite my great age, do you mean? Remember, darling girl, I was a child bride and you were born less than a year after I was wed.'

Lydia returned and dropping to her knees, embraced her mother. 'I love you, Mama. I meant no disrespect.' She scrambled up and shook her head. 'If I was as beautiful as you, I expect I should already be married myself.'

'My dear, do not fish for compliments. Although your hair is brown, your eyes are fine and your figure exemplary. You are a beautiful young lady and well you know it. If you had been able to make your come-out two years ago you might well have been a mother by now.'

'Good grief! That is a sobering thought, Mama. However, as the only child you produced was me in seventeen years of marriage, I might not be obliged to bear a child so soon or as frequently as some of your friends.'

'This is not a suitable conversation, Lydia, for an unmarried girl. I am shocked by your lack of decorum. Lady Alice is not a good influence on you, I fear. She is a flighty young miss and it is high time her father stepped in and found her a serious husband.'

'We have decided not to accept any offer of matrimony before we reach our majority — therefore we have a further two years to enjoy our freedom.' Lydia headed for the drawing room door, determined to escape before her mother would take issue with her outrageous statement.

She hurried across the spacious vestibule and almost ran up the stairs. Alice had promised to visit this afternoon and help with the selection of her ensemble. Her friend was also an only daughter, but not an only child, as she had three much older brothers. The earl and his countess had been surprised, but delighted, at the unexpected arrival of a girl after a gap of ten years. Consequently, Alice had grown up petted and spoilt by her adoring family.

Whatever the reasons for Alice's somewhat wild behaviour, Lydia loved her dearly and did her best to restrain the worst of her excesses. She smiled as she recalled the almost-elopement two years ago — she had been obliged to lock her friend in a closet to prevent her creeping out to meet her erstwhile husband. The young man in question had been an impecunious younger son — harmless enough, but quite unsuitable for Alice.

The autumn sun flooded into her

parlour, making the highly polished furniture glow and the crystal drops in the small chandelier sparkle. She headed for her bedchamber and called out to her maid. 'Jenny, what have you found for me? Do I have anything suitable for the assembly?'

The girl appeared from the dressing room, her arms full of gowns. 'You have four, Miss Lydia, that might do. I can soon add a ruffle or two if you want me to copy the latest fashion plates in *La Belle Assemblée*.'

'I cannot abide frills and so intend to ignore that trend.' Jenny draped the garments across the bed. 'I had forgotten I had so many to choose from.' She picked up an evening dress in the finest forget-me-not blue tulle. 'I have never worn this one, Jenny. It is perfect — the neckline is not too daring and the little blue flowers set it off perfectly. I believe I have gloves, slippers, reticule and fan to match.'

'And you have the sapphire parure left to you by your grandmother, Lady

Richmond,' Jenny said.

'I think sapphires would be too much for a local ball, Jenny. Perhaps I can find a ribbon to match the forget-me-nots around the hem and neck and thread it through my hair? I'm almost certain Miss Maidstone said she was expecting a new delivery of haberdashery last week.' Lydia looked at the mantel clock. There was ample time to walk into the village and make a purchase and still be home in time for her friend's visit. 'Jenny, please find my walking boots. We shall go at once and buy the ribbon we need.'

* * *

The walk to the village was no more than a mile and was accomplished without mishap. The pavements were busy with like-minded shoppers. There was a small gathering of excited young ladies standing in front of the assembly hall. Lydia hurried over to see what all the commotion was about.

One of the group, the cherries on her bonnet bobbing dangerously, rushed over to greet her. 'Miss Richmond, have you heard the news? A cavalry regiment is to be billeted in the empty barracks at Weeley. Imagine that! Our very own regiment of officers close by.'

'Miss Collins, how very exciting. I wonder if they will be in residence in time to attend the assembly ball next week?'

The young ladies exclaimed in delight at the thought of having a surplus of handsome young men to dance with instead of the usual lacklustre local gentlemen.

Another girl clapped her hands and spun, sending the skirt of her pastel green muslin swirling, and revealing more of her ankles than was seemly. 'Do you have tickets, Miss Richmond?'

'I do indeed, Miss Rushton. I was already eagerly anticipating the event, but now I'm almost beside myself.' Lydia put on a suitably excited expression. These girls were not close friends, but mere acquaintances, the daughters of local gentry, and did not move in the same stifling atmosphere as herself and Alice. They had no maids in attendance and were allowed to come and go from their homes as they pleased. She wished she was allowed such freedom.

'I wonder if the duke will favour us with an appearance? Mama told me he has a house party at the moment — some gentlemen and their ladies down for the shooting. Do tell us, Miss Richmond, if they are to come.' The speaker, a pretty girl in a pink striped walking dress, clutched her bosom and stared, starry-eyed, at Lydia.

The gathering completely blocked the pathway and a disgruntled matron clucked and tutted as she was obliged to step into the street in order to pass by.

'I am not privy to the movements of the Duke of Stenning. He is our neighbour and was a friend of my father's. I don't believe I've spoken to him this past two months.' She shook her head. 'And anyway, I don't believe he has ever attended an assembly ball, so why should he do so now?'

A sigh of disappointment rippled around the circle but then Miss Collins, ever a pragmatist, laughed gaily. 'He is way above *our* touch, but we shall have a dozen or more officers to dance with. There's nothing I like better than a military gentleman.'

'Pray excuse me, ladies. I have still to go to the haberdashers and must hurry, as I'm expecting a visitor this afternoon.'

The girls politely stepped aside, allowing Lydia and Jenny to pass. The babble of their chatter followed her into the cool interior of the shop. There were three customers being attended to by smartly dressed assistants but there was no sign of the proprietor. However, Miss Maidstone emerged immediately and greeted Lydia with a small curtsy and a smile.

'Good morning, Miss Richmond.

How can I help you today?'

Less than twenty minutes later Lydia was on her way home, delighted to have found an exact match for the forget-me-nots sewn to her ball gown. She nodded and smiled at several acquaintances who didn't stop to pass the time of day. Fortunately the gaggle of girls had moved elsewhere, no doubt to discuss at length the arrival of the regiment.

Usually she chatted to Jenny when they were out together, but today she wished to mull over something that had been said to her earlier. When she had denied speaking to the duke, she had told a falsehood. His grace visited at least once a week, usually to impart some local news to her mother or offer advice on her investments. Although she was usually present, she rarely spoke directly to him herself.

He was nearer her mother's age than hers, and although scrupulously polite and unfailingly charming, she found him unnerving and difficult to converse with. He was a formidable man, standing more than two yards high, and his shoulders were extremely broad. He wore his dark hair short, an uncompromising style which suited his demeanour. He treated her more as a child than a woman grown and she was grateful for this. Being teased and talked down to meant she was not expected to join in the conversation and thus show her ignorance of adult matters.

Her lips curved as she recalled the last time they had met. He had ridden over on his latest acquisition, a magnificent bay stallion, and had invited her to give an opinion on the animal. She had been about to go inside after a brisk walk around the lake. Her face had been hot, her hem mired and her boots muddy — hardly an appealing sight. She had mumbled something complimentary and scuttled in like a frightened rabbit. His laughter had followed her and she didn't blame him one jot for finding her a figure of fun.

On her return she ran upstairs to remove her gloves and bonnet and replace her walking boots with indoor slippers before hurrying down to the drawing room to share the exciting news. She burst in only to find her mother was not alone.

The duke stood and greeted her affectionately. 'Miss Richmond, what a delightful surprise. I understood from her ladyship that you had gone to the village.' His expression was bland but she could see amusement dancing in his eyes.

'I am back now, your grace . . . ' She faltered and her cheeks suffused with colour. Why was it she always sounded like a pea goose when speaking to him?

'Indeed you are, my dear, and looking quite delightful too.' He raised an eyebrow and glanced at a sofa, reminding her that etiquette demanded he remain on his feet until she was seated. Drat the man!

Ignoring his comment, she dropped

beside her mother, intending to tell her the good news. 'Mama, you will never guess what I was told in the village.'

'Lydia, my love, your news must wait. We have far more pressing matters to discuss.'

What could possibly be more important than the arrival of the cavalry regiment? She bit back her pert reply and tried to look interested. 'Yes, Mama, what is it you wish to tell me that also involves our guest?' She risked a glance in his direction and wished she hadn't. He was not impressed by her comment.

'The duke's sister, Lady Margaret Dunwoody, has offered to bring you out. Is that not kind of her? With your dear papa so recently deceased I cannot face the hustle and bustle of Town at the moment, so without this help you would not get your season at all.'

'Thank you, sir. I do appreciate Lady Margaret offering to sponsor me in March. However, I have no wish to leave my mother to gad about in

London. Having attended several informal parties this summer, I believe that I can be considered *out* already.'

Who was the more astonished by her statement was hard to tell. Her mother was rendered speechless and the duke's eyes widened in shock. He recovered first.

'Stuff and nonsense! Lady Richmond will manage perfectly well in your absence, as well you know. All young ladies want to have a season in Town. You are no different.'

Lydia was on her feet incensed by his assumption that he knew her motives. 'I beg your pardon, your grace, but I disagree. You have no right to dictate my movements, for you are not a member of my family.' She glared at him and he glared right back. 'Lord Richmond is arriving next week to take up his responsibilities as head of the household and my legal guardian. It is to him that I shall defer and not to — '

A choking sound coming from the sofa gave her pause. Her mother was about to explode. Lydia had never seen her parent so angry. Not waiting for the tirade to descend on her head, she moved rapidly for the open door. Her heart was hammering against her ribs. She could scarcely breathe. What could have possessed her to speak so intemperately?

Mama would have her return if she could find her. Therefore she would not go to her apartment, but hide in the maze until the coast was clear. She hurtled through the house and out through the garden-room and on to the terrace that ran around the south side of the building.

She was gasping for breath when she catapulted into the welcome darkness of the ancient maze. There was a small summer house in the centre where she could wait out the storm in comfort. She had played in this place so often as a child that she could instinctively find her way in any direction and had no recourse to take the flag from the stand in with her. Strangers were advised to wave this when they became hopelessly lost amidst the greenery.

The sun no longer shone into the maze and the summer house was not as welcoming as she had hoped. She wished she'd had the forethought to collect a wrap before she'd dashed out here. Mama should have calmed down within half an hour — surely she could sit here comfortably for such a short period of time? She was in the process of brushing off the debris from the wooden seat when there was a slight noise behind her.

She turned, expecting to find a squirrel or a bird. Instead, the duke stood there. He did not look at all friendly.

'Your grace, what are you doing here? Did my mother send you to ring a peal over me?'

He stepped forward and loomed over her. 'No, Miss Richmond. I am here on my own business.' He gestured to the bench. 'Shall we be seated?'

Feeling decidedly foolish, Lydia squashed

herself into the farthest corner, praying he would leave a suitable gap between them. 'I apologise if I offended you, sir, but — '

'You offended your mother, young lady, which is far more serious. In my opinion you have been overindulged and it is high time someone took you in hand.'

She stiffened and pressed her back hard against the wall. 'How I behave is none of your concern, sir. I have a perfectly satisfactory guardian who is quite content with my behaviour.' This was the second time she had referred to her uncle in this way — no doubt he would be surprised to discover he was expected to take an active role in her life. Mama had insisted after the funeral that there was no need for any interference from him.

The duke stretched out his long legs and examined the toes of his immaculate Hessians for non-existent dust. The silence stretched. Why didn't the wretched man say something? Then he swivelled and pinned her with his arctic blue gaze. 'Miss Richmond, my sister offered to sponsor you out of the kindness of her heart. She has her own progeny to launch but was prepared to give up her valuable time on your behalf. Yet you chose to toss it back as if it is of no importance.' He paused and Lydia wondered if she was expected to comment. He frowned and she drew breath to speak but reconsidered.

'Why in God's name would you turn down an offer any debutante in the land would be thrilled to have?'

2

Lydia recovered her composure. 'I have no wish to be paraded like a horse at Tattersall's and inspected by rich gentlemen on the lookout for a bride. Indeed, Your Grace, Lady Alice and I have decided we have no interest in matrimony at the moment. Therefore we are both perfectly content to enjoy our spinsterhood in our own neighbourhood.' It might be better not to mention the arrival of the regiment just now.

If she had announced she was a supporter of Napoleon Bonaparte he could not have been more surprised. He stared at her for several seconds before gathering his wits and finding an answer. 'Devil take it! Have you taken leave of your senses? Not wish to marry?' In his agitation he stood up and glowered at her. 'What else do you intend to do with your life? Making a suitable marriage is what young ladies strive for — what they are trained for from infancy.'

'Neither my nor Lady Alice's mama are in any hurry for us to wed. Therefore — '

'That is because you are both over-indulged and allowed to behave as you will. My dear girl, flitting about the countryside behaving like a village maiden might well ruin any chance you have of making an advantageous match. No, don't poker up at me, child. You know what I say is true.'

She leant forward, eager to explain her position. 'That is fustian, sir, and you know it. Lady Alice is the daughter of an earl and I of a peer. We are both heiresses and although I could not be considered a diamond of the first water, Lady Alice certainly is.'

His eyes narrowed and for an awful moment she thought he was going to approach her. She cowered back against the wall but he turned away to stand with his back towards her. She scrambled up, intending to reinforce her position with further evidence, but he swung round, raking her from head to toe with a disdainful look.

'I stand corrected, Miss Richmond. An attractive young lady of impeccable breeding, and a considerable fortune, will always be able to find herself a good husband.' His smile was not reflected in his eyes. 'I can assure you that a young lady with no reputation, however well connected, rich and beautiful, will be shunned by all gentlemen.'

Without waiting for her reaction to this outrageous statement, he strode off into the maze. He carried no flag, and she hoped he would become hopelessly lost and require her assistance to escape. She, of course, would refuse and leave him to fume within the leafy confines until rescued by a gardener.

She hurried to the entrance and to her chagrin, saw him striding across the grass towards the stables. Botheration!

Why was it he always bested her in their arguments and confrontations? Something else occurred to her as she slipped back unnoticed into the house and returned to her apartment. The duke must be thirty, if not older. Why was he not married already? There were not that many unattached dukes in the entire kingdom, so how was it that he had escaped being caught by a hopeful debutante? He must be the most eligible bachelor on the market. She was certain that even if he were old and ugly, some scheming matron should have entrapped him by now.

Did he have a deep and dark secret that prevented him from marrying? She shivered. Had he a mad wife locked in the attic? What nonsense! She was being fanciful — had been reading too many Gothic romances lately. Perhaps he suffered from an unrequited love and was determined not to marry anyone apart from the lady in question. The fact that he had two younger brothers meant there was no urgency for him to provide an heir. Anyway, whatever he did was none of her business.

She flopped on to the chaise longue in her parlour, intending to read the new novel she'd acquired from the circulating library. But before she had time to open the book the door burst open.

'Lydia, whatever did you say to His Grace to make him so agitated? He stormed off without saying farewell.'

'Mama, I just thanked him for his offer and said I had no interest in finding a husband at the moment.' Lydia swung her feet to the floor and made room for her mother to sit down. 'I cannot imagine what he found so upsetting about that. Did he, perhaps, promise Papa he would take an interest in my well-being?'

Her mother settled beside her before answering. 'He certainly made a promise of some sort to your father, but I was not privy to the contents of that vow. Sometimes I wish he was less punctilious in his attentions to us — being visited so often by a duke is a worry. I swear sometimes, my dear, I can think of nothing sensible to say to him.'

'In which case, Mama, can you not discourage him? I find him a difficult gentleman, high in the instep, and he always treats me as if I were a schoolroom miss.'

Her mother chuckled and patted her knee. 'Well, to him that is what you are. Don't forget, my love, that he has known you since you were no more than twelve years of age. He returned from his sojourn in the colonies and India when his father died. I recall — '

'Pray don't remind me. He arrived in all pomp and ceremony in his fine carriage to watch me sail over the fence, having been tossed from the back of Papa's new stallion.'

'He jumped down and carried you in with complete disregard for the fact that you were covered in mud and grass. What a bedraggled miss you were, to be sure.'

'Indeed I was. Although embarrassed to be seen in such a state, I was relieved the duke's appearance meant Papa was not able to chastise me as I deserved.'

A knock on the door interrupted their conversation. A footman announced the arrival of Lady Alice. Lydia rushed over to embrace her friend. 'Alice, I am so glad to see you . . .'

Alice returned her kiss, then curtsied politely to her mother. 'I bid you good day, Lady Richmond. I have a note for you from my mama.' She delved into her reticule and produced a folded square carefully sealed with a blob of red wax.

'I am delighted to see you, Lady Alice. I shall leave you to catch up on your gossip. Shall I have refreshments sent here, Lydia, or are you coming down to eat?'

'Thank you, Mama, but if you don't object I should prefer to remain here. Alice is going to help me choose my ensemble for the assembly next week.'

No sooner had the door closed behind her parent than Alice clapped her hands in glee. 'Have you heard? The regiment is already here and I've been told on good authority a dozen or more handsome young officers have bought tickets for the ball.'

'I knew they were coming, but not that they had arrived. Imagine having a surfeit of partners to choose from and not being obliged to stand up with gentlemen twice our age. We must take special care with our appearance, Alice, for I'm very sure that every other young lady in the vicinity will be doing so.'

'But we are the daughters of aristocracy — we shall have the pick of the bunch.'

Lydia giggled. 'You are quite outrageous. There are half a dozen girls prettier than I, and Miss Rushton, I believe you must admit, is the most beautiful young lady in the county.'

'That's as may be, but a well-bred

heiress trumps a lovely squire's daughter.' Alice whirled around the room like a child. 'We shall have the pick of the officers. I intend to have at least three at my beck and call. Papa will be so cross — he's still hoping your duke will offer for me.'

'Lord Stenning is not *my duke*! He was a friend of my father's and continues to take an interest in our family.' She curled up on the day bed and patted the end, indicating her friend should be seated too. 'His older sister, Lady Margaret, is staying with him and has offered to sponsor me next season. I refused of course — why should I go to London when a regiment of cavalry officers has come here?'

By the time Alice departed Lydia was satisfied that she had selected the perfect ensemble for the coming ball. Her friend had been suitably impressed by her determination to remain at Ravenscroft. She wasn't entirely comfortable with Alice's intention to have several officers dance attendance on her. Sometimes she was forced to agree with her mother that her friend was a trifle wild, but she would never admit this out loud. If she did so, Mama might insist the connection was severed and she wasn't about to give up her bosom friend for anyone.

★　★　★

The days flew past and finally the time had come to prepare for the ball. Jenny surpassed herself and Lydia was delighted with her appearance. 'This colour is so pretty, and the ribbon perfect threaded through my hair.'

'I am sure you will be the belle of the ball, miss. The sapphire pendant you have threaded on the ribbon complements your outfit.'

Lydia collected her matching reticule and fan and waited whilst her abigail placed her evening cloak around her shoulders. She was ready and eager to leave. Downstairs her mama was waiting impatiently.

29

'There you are at last, my love. We must not keep the horses standing any longer.'

'I beg your pardon, mama. I think we both look splendid. We could be sisters, could we not?'

Her mother smiled and shook her head. 'I have no wish to be taken as your sister; I am proud to be your parent. Now, come along. I wish to arrive in time to secure chairs near the dancing.'

Outside the night was clear and cold, perfect for an evening excursion in October. A footman handed them into the carriage and folded the steps away. They were not taking maids tonight; the occasion was so close to home they could return if anything untoward occurred.

In the darkness of the interior Lydia smoothed out the skirt of her gown, surprised to discover her fingers were trembling. Was the thought of meeting a handsome officer unnerving her?

'Mama, there will be cavalry officers

at the Assembly Hall tonight. I intend to dance with as many as I can.'

Her mother sighed. 'Oh dear! I have no wish for you to appear flighty, Lydia. You may dance every dance, but remember you must not stand up with the same gentleman more than once. And you certainly may not waltz. Is that quite clear?'

'I promise I shall not disgrace you. I know young ladies are not allowed to waltz until they are given permission. When will you allow me to take part in this new dance?'

'At Almacks the patronesses frown upon unmarried girls taking part. I know we are in the country, but I think it better that you don't participate tonight. After all, you are to attend Lady Alice's name day ball next month — perhaps I shall give my permission for you to waltz then.'

With this Lydia had to be content. She hoped Lady Bellamy could be persuaded to include some officers on the guest list. The carriage lurched to a stop outside the handsome red-brick building in which the assembly rooms were housed. She wanted to lean forward and peer from the window like a child but managed to restrain herself.

The door was opened and the steps let down. 'Good heavens, Mama — they have put down a red carpet and there are a dozen or more flambeaux lit on either side. I know I have only attended three such occasions, so I'm not sure, but surely this is most unusual?'

Her mother descended first, exclaiming in delight when she saw what had been done. 'You are quite right to be surprised, my love. I don't remember such a thing being done before.'

Lydia's excitement drained away through her dainty dancing slippers. She was obliged to clutch the door to steady herself. There could be only one explanation for this show of splendour: someone very important was to attend the ball. The only person she could think of in the vicinity was the Duke of

Stenning. Why should he choose to make an appearance tonight of all nights? After his scathing comments in the maze about the possibility of losing her reputation, she would now be unable to enjoy herself with a handsome cavalry captain without being aware of his disapproving face watching her every move.

'You are wool-gathering, child. We cannot dally here; there are other carriages arriving behind us and we are holding up the guests.'

Lydia apologised and fell into step beside her mother. They were bowed into the spacious vestibule by two footmen, and two maids stepped forward to take their dominoes. There was no time to say what she suspected, for she was whisked across the floor and into the ballroom.

The chamber was already half full; and amidst the swirl of young ladies dressed in similar fashion and gentlemen in formal eveningwear, Lydia saw a dozen or more red coats. Her heart raced, the bodice of her gown became unaccountably tight, and a thrill of excitement rippled from her toes to her crown.

'Thank goodness — Lady Bellamy has secured places for us. Come along, my dear; we must take our chairs before another group steals them away.'

As Lydia threaded her way through the press of people she smiled and nodded to those she was acquainted with. She could not help but be aware of the admiring glances she received from more than one of the officers. She was not familiar with being stared at by handsome young gentlemen and was a trifle flustered by the time she reached their destination.

Alice squealed and jumped to her feet. 'At last! I had quite given you up. Such excitement — Lady Ponsonby has put out the red carpet to match the officers. You created quite a stir as you came across the room, Lydia. I'm sure you will be surrounded by eager partners as soon as the orchestra is ready to play the first cotillion.'

Lydia drew her friend to one side until they were hidden behind a marble column. 'The carpet and all the fuss is not for them. I fear that the duke and his party are to attend tonight. It is unprecedented and so must warrant all this ostentation.'

'Do you think so?' Alice looked around the ballroom at the fluttering and chattering groups, all of which were ignoring the soldiers and staring avidly at the double doors in expectation. 'I do believe you're correct. Most of the guests would not have had the opportunity to brush shoulders with someone so top-lofty. One might think the Prince Regent was to come, not a mere duke.'

'He is the most eligible bachelor in the kingdom, and he is making an appearance here, of all places. Of course all the matchmaking mamas will be anxious to present their daughters in the hope that he takes an interest.'

'Imagine the honour of being the first to dance with him — I do hope he chooses one of us, don't you?'

This was the last thing Lydia hoped but she could hardly reveal her feelings on the subject to her friend. 'He will probably stare down his aristocratic nose at all of us and dance with no one, unless they are a member of his party.'

'Lady Alice, Lydia, please don't lurk behind the pillar in that way. It is most unladylike. Come and join us until the music starts.'

'Yes, Mama. I apologise. Lady Alice and I have been discussing the likelihood of our neighbour and his guests appearing at the ball tonight. We cannot think of any other reason for the red carpet, can you?'

Lydia and her friend selected two gilt chairs beside their mamas and stood behind them; it would not do to sit and spoil the hang of their gowns.

'His Grace has not visited since you were so impolite to him the other day, so I have no notion if you are correct. I cannot imagine why he should wish to come tonight; he has never attended such an event before.'

A collective murmur of expectation travelled around the ballroom. All heads turned towards the doors. Lydia held her breath. Striding into the room was the unmistakable figure of the duke. He stood a head taller than most men and was able to see across the crowd. He paused in the doorway to allow his party to catch up with him. He was accompanied by three gentlemen and two ladies; all were dressed in the height of fashion that made everyone in the room feel shabby.

His hawk-like gaze scanned the press of people as if looking for someone in particular. He stepped forward, nodding and smiling as other guests greeted him, but not stopping to converse. Alice clutched her hand.

'He is coming here!'

Lydia's mother arrived at her side. 'Your Grace, how delightful to see you.' She dipped in a graceful curtsy and Lydia followed suit.

'Lady Richmond, Miss Richmond, I

was hoping to see you here.' Alice and her mother also curtsied and he responded politely with a small bow. 'Allow me to introduce to you my sister, Lady Margaret Dunwoody, and her husband Lord Dunwoody.' More bows and bobs followed. Next he introduced the other members of his party as his two younger brothers and the young lady as the sister of Lord Dunwoody.

Formalities completed, Lydia expected him to move away but, to her consternation, he remained. How were she and Alice to achieve their goal of dancing every dance if he stood beside them, glowering at anyone who had the temerity to approach?

3

The orchestra squawked and the master of ceremonies stepped forward to announce that the first dance would be a country dance. This meant that five or more couples would be required to make up a set. Lydia and Alice edged away from the quietly conversing group made up of the Stenning party, her mother and Lady Bellamy.

'We must make sure the officers know we are available to dance. We shall never get a partner if we remain here,' Alice whispered.

'I would not mind if any of *his* party seemed inclined to dance themselves. Why come to a ball if you have no wish to participate in the dancing?' She had barely finished speaking when they were surrounded by a sea of red. These gentlemen were accompanied by the master of ceremonies, who must introduce them before they could accept a request for a dance.

Lydia could scarcely take in the names and ranks of those before her. She didn't offer her hand but nodded and dipped as each one was introduced. Alice had already departed to join a set with a golden-haired Adonis who she thought might be a captain, but she had missed his name entirely.

Another young man, a Lieutenant Boothroyd, bowed and held out his arm. Lydia was about to take it when, to her astonishment, she was prevented from doing so.

'I believe this is my dance, Miss Richmond.' The duke held out his arm and she had no option but to place her gloved hand upon it. The group of eager cavalry officers had already vanished into the crowd to seek available young ladies.

She had recovered her composure by the time they reached the head of the set. The six other couples had moved down in order to accommodate their

40

arrival. 'Your Grace, I did not know that you danced.'

He smiled down at her. 'I am not in my dotage, my dear. I am one-and-thirty, perfectly capable of joining in a *contredanse*. Now, I do hope you are proficient, as I should hate to be embarrassed in front of so many interested spectators.'

'I am considered light on my feet, Your Grace. We shall see who is the most proficient at the end of the dance.'

There was no more time to talk as the orchestra struck up the tune, and from that point forward she was too busy concentrating on the steps to bandy words with her partner. It wasn't until they had danced with all the couples and were promenading to resume their place at the head of the set that Lydia glanced at her partner.

'At last! I was beginning to think you were deliberately ignoring me, Miss Richmond.' He was smiling at her.

She returned his smile. 'I do beg your pardon, sir, but after my immodest claim to be an excellent dancer, I fear I was obliged to concentrate in order not to disgrace myself — or you.'

'If I am honest, my dear, I found the whole proceeding unnecessarily strenuous. Shall we abandon the dance and take a stroll around the extremities of this building?'

'We cannot do that — only in a dire emergency is one allowed to leave the set.'

'What would be considered a dire emergency?'

'Well, I suppose if my hem was coming down because my partner had stepped on it — ' she was having difficulty hiding her amusement. This was a nonsensical conversation and not at all in character for the austere Duke of Stenning.

Before she could prevent him, he pretended to stumble and trod heavily on her gown, causing her to lurch sideways in a most unladylike manner. 'Miss Richmond, how clumsy of me. I have torn your beautiful gown. You must immediately retire from the dance.' His expression was suitably contrite but his eyes were full of mischief.

Lydia did not know whether to be furious at his deliberate destruction of her dress or impressed by his determination to achieve his ends. She carefully gathered up the ruined hem and draped it over her arm. 'This *was* my favourite ensemble, Your Grace, and — '

'My dear Miss Richmond, we are making a spectacle of ourselves standing here. Allow me to escort you to the ladies' retiring room so that you may have your gown repaired.'

He was quite correct — the tabbies, sitting around the edge of the dance floor on the little gilt chairs, were already whispering and nodding in their direction. Fortunately her own mother was too busy talking to Lady Bellamy and had not noticed the contretemps.

He whisked her through the press of people and into the cool of the vestibule. The room she needed was upstairs. 'Thank you, Your Grace. I shall make my own way from here.' She examined the tear more closely and her eyes filled. The damage was so severe that she had no alternative but to return home. 'This cannot be repaired. Would you be so kind as to have my carriage fetched?'

'Devil take it! I have ruined your evening and that was not my intention.' He snapped his fingers and a footman appeared at his side. He spoke too softly for her to hear what he said. She must send another minion to inform Mama of the accident. There was no need for anyone else to miss the ball — she would return on her own. She delved into her reticule and removed her handkerchief.

He turned back, his face serious. 'I must apologise for using improper language in front of you. Please, little one, don't cry. You live such a short distance away; surely you can return and change into another gown and come back to enjoy the remainder of the evening?'

Sadly, she shook her head. 'I do not have another ball gown ready, Your Grace. There has been no necessity. I must send for my cloak and make sure Lady Richmond is aware that I've gone home.'

He was staring over her head and nodded. 'Excellent. My carriage is here, and so is your domino.' He took it from the girl and shook it out before draping it around Lydia's shoulders. 'Come along, child. I shall escort you back to Ravenscroft.'

He gave her no time to protest, but encircled her waist and hurried her across the hall and out into the crisp autumn evening. Somehow she found herself inside his magnificent coach with him sitting opposite as if there was nothing untoward about the situation at all.

Lydia closed her eyes, trying to understand what had just happened. The duke should not have come with her — there would be those who would think he was showing her a particular interest by doing so.

'Miss Richmond, I shall make this up to you, I give you my word — '

She interrupted him, something she would not have considered doing until this evening. 'Thank you, Your Grace, but there is no need. Your intention was to remove us from the set, not to ruin my gown. I accept your apology on that count; however, I am at a loss to know what possessed you to accompany me.' His face was invisible in the darkness but his reaction was so sudden she recoiled on the squabs. He jolted upright and the vehicle rocked violently.

'Are you suggesting there is something improper about my actions?' His voice was icy, his words clipped.

How dare he speak to her like that when *he* was in the wrong? 'We are unchaperoned. In case you might not have noticed, Your Grace, I am an unmarried lady and you are an unmarried gentleman.' She had intended to say no more but she was so incensed she could not stop herself. 'Or perhaps you consider yourself above the normal rules, Your Grace? Can a duke do as he pleases and no one think ill of him?' She was sure she could hear his teeth grinding. He certainly was breathing rather heavily.

'Miss Richmond, I do believe you are suggesting I have compromised you. I do hope you're not expecting me to make you an offer?' His words were soft but his anger was barely contained.

From somewhere deep inside she found the courage to answer. 'Yes, that is what I am saying. However, I can assure you, sir, that even if my reputation is in tatters I should not accept an offer from you. You are an arrogant, objectionable, dictatorial — '

To her astonishment he laughed. 'Enough, little firebrand. Your message has been received and understood. We are of the same mind, Miss Richmond. Matrimony between us is out of the question.'

Her heart was making a valiant

attempt to escape through her rib cage. She clutched her reticule and attempted to breathe slowly through her nose. What had possessed her to speak so intemperately? Should she apologise or pretend the words unspoken?

'In which case, sir, how do you intend to silence the gossip? You can be very sure that our departure together has been noted and will be the main topic of discussion at the assembly rooms.'

'There is something you are not aware of, my dear. Your father entrusted me with your welfare. Your uncle is not your legal guardian; I am.'

'I don't believe you. You are all but a stranger to us — why should Papa have done such a thing ... ' Her voice faltered. As her father and his brother had been estranged for years, it was very likely he had arranged things in this manner. 'I beg your pardon, Your Grace, you must understand this is a great shock to me. Lord Richmond is coming to stay and I believed it was to take up his responsibilities at last.'

The carriage rocked as he shifted in the darkness and to her horror arrived by her side on the seat. 'There are other things of which you are not privy. I had hoped to be able to tell you when you were living under my roof — but I have no choice. I believe I must tell you everything tonight.'

Lydia peered into the darkness. The moon was full and she could see quite clearly they were not travelling down her drive but somewhere else entirely. Was she being abducted?

'Where are you taking me? I wish to go home right now. I don't care what you arranged with Papa; I will never accept you as my guardian.' Even to her ears she sounded petulant and hysterical — small wonder he kept referring to her as a child. She tried to steady her breathing, but his closeness was unnerving her.

'Don't be silly, my dear. You have been reading too many Gothic novels and are allowing your imagination run away with you. You know the way we're going — to Stenning. I refuse to hold a serious conversation whilst in a carriage.' His gloved hand rested briefly on hers. 'Sit still and don't fret. Everything will be revealed to you as soon as we are there.'

The carriage swung sideways as it turned into the imposing gate of Stenning Hall. She bit her lip and tried to remain composed. So many questions were chasing themselves through her head that she was dizzy with it all. Did Mama know of this arrangement? If what he said was true, then why hadn't he made his position clear eighteen months ago? Lord Richmond must know he wasn't the head of the household — was this why he'd not visited?

The carriage jolted to a halt and a bevy of footmen arrived to lower the steps and escort their master into his magnificent house. He slid smoothly past her and held up his hand. She ignored him and was about to step down unaided, quite forgetting she had a gown with a trailing hem. Her front foot went through the rip and she tumbled forward.

By some miracle he was able to catch her before she hit the ground. His arms were like bands of steel around her waist and he swung her around and gently returned her to her feet. Unfortunately she was still unsteady from the fall and this caused her to ram her right foot through the material so that she was trapped within its folds. When he released his hold on her she would surely fall again. Without thinking, she clutched his arms. 'Oh dear! How stupid of me, Your Grace, but I find myself quite unable to walk. If you would kindly — '

Before she could complete the request she was in the air again and held fast against his chest. 'You goose — of course you cannot walk with your foot through your gown. I shall carry you inside. No, sweetheart, do not wriggle; I should hate to drop you.

These steps are made of marble and unpleasantly hard.'

Her face was scarlet as he marched past his servants and into the vast chequered vestibule. She tugged at his lapel and hissed between clenched teeth. 'Put me down at once. I have no wish to be carried around like a parcel.'

Instead he shouldered his way into one of the many chambers on the ground floor and gently restored her to her feet. 'Don't try and remove your foot yourself, Miss Richmond, sit down and I shall do it for you.'

In desperation she attempted to kick her leg free and the sound of ripping silk echoed around the room. She had been successful — but at what cost?

'Botheration! I have turned a mishap into a total disaster.' The remains of her skirt hung in tatters around her legs, revealing her petticoats. Hastily she collapsed on to a padded chair, tucking the remains of her gown around her ankles.

He shook his head in disbelief. 'You nincompoop. Now that gown is beyond repairing. You will have to remain here until something else has been fetched from Ravenscroft.'

There was no need for him to tell her how stupid she had been. If *he* had not made such an improper suggestion *she* would not have taken such a drastic action.

'Perhaps Lady Margaret might have something I could borrow? I have no wish to stay here any longer than necessary.'

He nodded curtly and strode across to pull the bell strap with such vigour that the bell would be clanging loudly in the servants' hall.

'You brought me here to tell me something, Your Grace. I should like to know what it is. I should also like to know — '

'Enough, Miss Richmond. I shall explain everything in good time. I have arranged for a chamber to be prepared for you. I suggest you retire for the night and we continue this discussion in the morning.'

The butler glided into the room and bowed. The duke explained the predicament and the elderly gentleman hurried away, carefully averting his eyes from her, presumably to summon a female servant. Moments later Taylor, the housekeeper, curtsied at the door.

'Miss Richmond, if you would care to accompany me I shall take you upstairs immediately.'

Lydia was careful to keep the remnants of her gown from flying apart as she stood up. She had nothing to say to the man who had so casually announced he had been her legal guardian since her father had passed away. He had turned his back, which allowed her to scurry after Taylor without fear of being embarrassed.

⋆　⋆　⋆

Aubrey waited until Lydia had gone before moving. This was an unmitigated disaster and it was entirely his fault. His intention had been to dance with her and by doing so, make her a success. Instead he had ruined her evening and possibly her reputation.

He cursed under his breath. The girl was scarcely out of the school room — far too young for him even if he was contemplating matrimony. Good Lord! He had known her since she was a child and the very thought of taking her to his bed was repellent. He could not marry her, so he must find another way out of this mess.

He poured himself a generous measure of brandy and took it to a chair beside the fire. Why hadn't he made it clear to her and her mother that he was the head of their household? If he had done so, this debacle would not have occurred. He frowned as he sipped the amber liquid. There must be a way he could put things right. Lydia had grown into her looks, and although some might consider her sharp-featured, the beauty of her eyes and her glorious red-brown hair more than compensated. He rubbed his fingers across his jaw — it was a damn nuisance his facial hair grew so fast that if he wished to remain clean-shaven, he had to seek his valet's attention twice a day.

Appearing unkempt was the least of his worries at the moment. He closed his eyes and stretched out his feet towards the blaze. He thought back to the day when Richmond had asked him to assume the responsibility for his wife and child in the event of his untimely death. Aubrey had agreed without hesitation; his friend had been no more than fifteen years his senior and as fit as an ox, and the likelihood of him actually having to assume this responsibility was remote.

Richmond's death in a riding accident had taken place whilst he was in the colonies on business matters. By the time he returned six months had passed, and when he called to see the widow and her daughter and offer his condolences, he immediately understood Lady

Richmond had not been informed of this arrangement. She naturally assumed her brother-in-law was Lydia's guardian. He had not wanted to disabuse her, so had maintained no more than a friendly interest in the household until circumstances changed.

Lydia had become a close friend of the flighty and over-indulged Lady Alice, and the two girls were beginning to get a reputation for being undisciplined. When he had learned of the arrival of a cavalry regiment, his heart had sunk to his boots. He had immediately written to his sister and asked for her assistance. He could do nothing about the behaviour of Lady Alice — that was none of his business — but he was both morally and legally obliged to ensure that his ward did not become embroiled in something unsavoury.

He swallowed the remainder from his glass and slammed it down on the side table. He had no option. However much he disliked the idea, he would have to offer for the chit and they would have to make the best of it. She was impeccably bred, had a sizeable fortune, and was pretty enough. He had avoided the parson's mousetrap for years, but had only himself to blame for his predicament. He had entrapped himself. He must return at once to the assembly rooms and speak to Lady Richmond.

4

Lydia insisted that she needed no help to disrobe and had no wish to be disturbed until morning. No sooner had the door closed behind the housekeeper than she blew out all the candles and slipped out behind her. She had no intention of spending the night here — Mama would be horrified, however legitimate the circumstances.

The wide passageway was deserted. She tiptoed along it and paused at the head of the enormous marble staircase. As she stood there in the shadows the duke appeared from the anteroom they had been in and vanished through the front door. The footman closed it after his master and then he too disappeared.

This was her opportunity to escape without being seen. There was no need to hold up the skirts of her gown as they flew freely around her ankles, in no way impeding her rapid progress. She raced across the vestibule, wrestled with the door, and escaped into the darkness unseen.

Despite her anxiety about her mission, Lydia's spirits lifted as she pulled the door closed behind her. She must not dally. Ravenscroft was a good half an hour walk in daylight; heaven knew how much longer it would take in the moonlight.

A sudden sound in the darkness forced her to stumble and scrape her hand on the masonry. A cold, damp nose pressed into her palm. 'Juno, silly dog, you scared me half to death. Are you coming with me? I trust you will behave yourself and not vanish down a rabbit hole as you did last week.'

The large brown dog, of indeterminate ancestry, licked her hand and his tail thumped heavily against her thigh. He was well known to her as he often accompanied his owner when he visited. Having him at her side was a definite bonus — in the unlikely event that she came across a poacher he would not dare approach her now. 'Come along, boy. I wish to get this journey completed and be safely in my bed before Mama returns.'

Her evening slippers were not ideal footwear for a jaunt through the countryside in the middle of the night. With the dog padding at her side, she set off briskly. It was no hardship to be out on such an evening and she was almost able to push aside the reason for her nocturnal escapade. Despite the nip in the air she was warm enough inside her evening cloak. However, when she scrambled over the stile that marked the boundary between Ravenscroft and her neighbour, she began to doubt whether her decision had been sensible.

What had possessed her to abscond from Stenning? Her disappearance would cause uproar and she had no wish to distress the duke's guests. As she drew closer to home she was horrified to see there were lights showing in some downstairs windows.

Botheration! Mama must have returned early from the ball. She had hoped to leave the difficult explanations until tomorrow.

There was little point in attempting to enter the building undetected — the place was fully illuminated and even from across the turning circle she could hear loud voices. Her slippers had disintegrated on the journey and she was limping badly. She hobbled up the steps and pushed open the front door.

'My darling girl, where have you been? I have been beside myself with worry. Heavens above! What has happened to you, child?' Her mother ran across the hall and Lydia flung herself into her open arms.

'Mama, I'm so sorry I worried you — '

'Hush, my love. We shall not talk about things now. Look at your feet! They are leaving bloodstains on the tiles. Can you manage to get upstairs to your apartment, or shall I send for the footman to carry you?'

Lydia had been transported quite enough for one evening so refused the offer. Once secure in the privacy of her bedchamber she told her mother about the extraordinary events of the evening. As her mother helped her undress and bathed her bleeding feet, she listened without comment. When Lydia had completed her tale her mother collapsed beside her on the bed.

'Before I can begin to contemplate the significance of your news, my love, I wish to know what prompted you to run away from Stenning Hall.'

'Mama, imagine what Lady Margaret and the rest of his family would think if they had found me, without a by-your-leave, sleeping at Stenning? Leaving so suddenly with His Grace from the ball must already be a source of speculation. By coming home as I did, we can pretend he brought me here. If he says otherwise we will deny it and suggest that he was foxed and cannot remember.'

'A laudable idea, Lydia, but I fear it

will not do. Both his staff and ours know the true facts and servants spread gossip like wildfire. Also, as far as I know, nobody has any knowledge of your unorthodox departure. I had no idea that you had gone for an hour or more, and then I was told that your gown had been irreparably damaged and you had returned home.'

'Did you not think it peculiar that our carriage was waiting for you?'

'No, my dear. I just assumed you had sent it back directly. There was no gossip about you and Sinclair having left together.' Her mother collected the supper tray from Lydia's parlour. 'I retract my previous statement. You being safely home, whatever any servant might say to the contrary, means your reputation is intact.'

Lydia discovered she was ravenous and devoured most of what had been sent up. When she was finished her mother placed the tray on a convenient side table. 'I wish I had left a note. Do you think anyone will discover my absence before the morning?'

'I very much doubt it; as soon as we are done here I shall write a letter to His Grace informing him what has transpired. I will request that he attends me here immediately. There are matters to be settled between us.'

'Mama, will we now have to reside with him? Is he to dictate our every move in future?'

'Absolutely not — he's your guardian, not mine. This is your home and here you shall remain until you are married.' She frowned. 'I cannot believe he is actually your guardian and not Lord Richmond. Why did he not tell us this last year when he returned from his business trip abroad?'

'I have no idea, Mama. No doubt all will be revealed when he visits tomorrow morning.'

*   *   *

Aubrey tried to make his return to the ball as inconspicuous as possible

— almost an impossible feat for a man of his stature. He was mingling with the throng, nodding and smiling, when someone caught his eye. Where the devil was Lady Richmond and her crony? He stepped into an alcove in order to check the dance floor. Lady Alice was dancing with a dashing young officer (as was to be expected) but no one from his party, nor Lady Richmond, was participating in the lively Scottish reel.

Then he spotted a doorway at the back of the hall from which a constant flow of ladies and gentlemen came and went. There must be a card room — he had seen the supper laid out elsewhere. He made his way to the door and entered. Sure enough, his house party were seated at a table playing a lively game of loo. He hoped the stakes were not set ruinously high, as Margaret's husband had a disastrous tendency to dip too deep.

He strolled across and stood behind his sister's shoulder. 'Do you know where Lady Richmond is hiding? I have urgent business with her.'

She placed her cards on the table and gestured for him to move away to a less crowded corner of the room. 'More to the point, Sinclair: where have you been for the past hour? After you trod on Miss Richmond's gown and quite ruined the poor girl's evening, you also vanished.'

He explained to her what had transpired. She stared at him as if he had run mad. 'Are you telling me you neglected to inform Lady Richmond that her daughter is your ward? What must they be thinking? This is an unmitigated disaster — '

'There's no need to tell me that, sister. I am only too aware that I must now offer for a young lady who has as little interest in marrying me as I do in becoming her husband.'

'We must return to Stenning at once — maybe we can avoid the necessity of you being obliged to make an offer. And, Sinclair, I can assure you that whatever Miss Richmond might have said to the contrary, she will be delighted to become your duchess. You are the most eligible bachelor in the country — indeed, my dear brother, if you were in your dotage she would still be thrilled with the arrangement.'

Their animated conversation was attracting the attention of the other players at her table. 'Finish your hand, Margaret, and then we will leave. I have yet to locate Lady Richmond. Even though I am the girl's legal guardian, I feel it's only right to ask her permission to pay my addresses to her daughter.'

While his sister finished her game he drifted around the card room, the ballroom and the supper room, but to no avail. Lady Richmond was quite definitely not there. She must have followed her daughter as soon as she learnt of her mishap. She would arrive at Ravenscroft expecting Miss Richmond to be there. God knew what conclusion she would draw from her daughter's absence. Even more reason to make the girl an offer. If he was honest, he accepted his sister's comment that Miss Richmond would be delighted to become his duchess — what girl wouldn't be?

Within half an hour his party was safely established in his carriage and trundling back to Stenning. The conversation was lively, but he remained silent, lost in contemplation of his future. He had not expected to inherit the title as he had an older brother — however, when James had died unexpectedly from the sweating fever, his life changed — and not for the better.

He had been obliged to give up his commission in the cavalry and return home. His father had made it quite clear that it would not do for the Marquis of Sinclair to be gallivanting around the country following Wellington. What was acceptable for a younger son was not acceptable for the heir. When his father had died three years ago Aubrey had been almost relieved to be able to take over the responsibility after kicking his heels in the old duke's shadow for so long.

He had decided then not to inflict the burden of being the eldest son of a duke on any child of his. He would remain unmarried. His physical needs were satisfied by his mistress, the widow of a baronet, whom he kept in a luxurious townhouse. Therefore, his brother was being groomed to take on the role when he kicked the bucket.

The drive to his home was short and the carriage was soon bowling along the immaculate drive and pulling up in front of the steps. He remained in his seat, allowing the two women to descend before he did. He caught up with Margaret in the vestibule. 'Miss Richmond has retired; unfortunately she has not brought with her the necessities for an overnight stay. Would you mind calling in on her and making sure she is happy with the items the housekeeper found for her?'

'I assume the items were mine? We are about the same height and build.'

She smiled. 'Don't look so worried, my dear. We shall come about, never fear. I heard nothing about you departing with the girl unchaperoned. I believe that your behaviour has not compromised her in any way — with luck Lady Richmond will not insist on you marrying the chit.' She turned to climb the stairs. 'I shall come back immediately and tell you how I find her. Why not wait for me in the yellow drawing-room? The others have gone to the billiard room so we shall be private there.'

There was barely time for him to pour himself a small glass of brandy before his sister entered. Her face was ashen and her hands were clutched dramatically to her bosom. 'The girl is not there. The bed not slept in. Sinclair, what was happened to her?'

★ ★ ★

Lydia, her injured feet clean and bandaged, was about to fall asleep

71

when someone knocking on the front door jolted her upright. For a moment she was disorientated, not sure where she was or what she was hearing, and then she remembered. There was only one person who could be demanding entry in the middle of the night — the duke had come looking for her. Mama must have forgotten to send him a note.

She tumbled out of bed, ignoring the discomfort from her injuries, and quickly pulled on her bed robe. Why was no one answering the door? She undid the latch on the window and threw it up. Her bedchamber over-looked the front door but she was unable to see who was standing in the shelter of the portico — however, there was an enormous horse grazing on the grass that bordered the turning circle.

'Your Grace, is that you? Please stop hammering on the door — you don't want to wake up the servants.'

Immediately the noise stopped and he appeared below her. 'Thank God! How the hell did you get here?'

'I walked, Your Grace. I thought it better not to remain under your roof.'

'I refuse to carry on a conversation in this ridiculous fashion — will you come down and let me in?'

She was about to refuse, then reconsidered. Far better to have him inside, than waking everyone and causing further scandal. Should she keep him kicking his heels whilst she dressed, or go down as she was?

'I shall continue to bang the knocker until you, or someone else, opens this door.'

'Very well, I shall come down, but I cannot open the front door on my own. You must go around to the garden room — I can unlock that easily enough.'

She hastily lit a taper from the embers in the fire and, with her candle held aloft, she ran through the house and into the glass-fronted room in which her father had once grown exotic plants. She could see an outline prowling up and down the terrace outside. This chamber smelt of neglect; indeed, she couldn't remember the last time she'd been in here herself. It had been Papa's domain and since his death she and her mother had all but forgotten about it.

The bolts on the outer door slid back noisily. Fortunately this structure had been added to the side of the building, and both the family bedchambers and staff quarters were on the other side.

'At last! What is that dreadful smell? Do you have a rodent problem?'

Well! How uncivil he was when she had just got out of bed especially to let him in. 'Your Grace, if you care to follow me we can go into Papa's study. No one ever goes in there, but Bennett has the chamber cleaned regularly. And I can assure you, sir, we do not have either rats or mice in this house. We have two excellent cats indoors and the terrier for the stable area.'

As he followed her, she noticed that he was remarkably light on his feet for such a large gentleman. The study was situated close by and required a journey of no more than a few yards. She pushed open the door and headed for the mantelpiece in order to light the candles. Soon the room was bathed in the flickering glow of half a dozen good wax candles.

'God's teeth! You are in your nightgown. Have you totally taken leave of your senses, Miss Richmond? What maggot got into your brain and persuaded you to come down as you are?'

This was the outside of enough! 'It is two o'clock in the morning — where else do you think I would be, but in my bed?' No sooner had she spoken than she realised she had made the matter worse. One should never mention one's bed to a gentleman under any circumstances. Too late to repine — she might as well complete the complaint. 'Your Grace, you are the one who was hammering on the door and demanding to be let in instantly. I have merely followed your instructions. It is you who have breached convention at every turn tonight.' She raised her hand and counted off his misdemeanours on her fingers. 'Firstly, you deliberately trod on my gown. Secondly, you abducted me and told me I had to remain at Stenning even though I had no overnight bag with me. Thirdly, you have — '

To her amazement he laughed. 'I think you have made your point admirably, my dear. I dread to think how long a list you have prepared for my edification.'

'At least another three items, sir. Are you sure you do not wish to hear them?'

'Absolutely not! I suppose us being in here unchaperoned like this makes what I have to say that much easier.'

Before she could protest he moved closer, took her hands and then dropped dramatically to one knee.

'Please, Your Grace, do not say it . . . '

'We have no choice, sweetheart. Now, be a good girl and remain silent whilst I get this proposal out of the way.' Her hands were all but invisible in his. His hold was gentle, so she attempted to remove them. Immediately his grip tightened. 'Miss Richmond, make me the happiest of men, and do me the estimable honour of becoming my duchess.'

5

Lydia shook her head. 'Thank you for your kind offer, Your Grace, but I cannot accept. We would not suit.'

Instead of releasing her he drew her closer. 'We must make the best of things, my dear. You would have had to accept a gentleman's proposal at some point — after all, a well-bred young lady has no other choice but to marry. You will not get a better offer.' He smiled affectionately and raised her clenched fists to his lips. He brushed each one in turn with his mouth; not exactly a kiss, but close enough.

'I have no desire to marry a duke — or indeed any other member of the aristocracy. When I do decide to get married it will be to a handsome young cavalry officer and definitely not to you.'

'A cavalry officer? Over my dead

body, my girl. Do not forget that I am your legal guardian until you are five-and-twenty — I can assure you I shall not entertain the request of any officer. A military life is not for you. You are better suited to be my bride — you will not be separated from your mother and I will allow you free rein to redecorate Stenning in whatever ridiculous fancy you have.' He smiled encouragingly. 'And you can replenish your wardrobe with the latest fashions and I shall open my townhouse for you in the season.'

Finally he released her hands and she moved away to curl up on a padded armchair. How could he think she would be swayed by the offer of new gowns and decorations? What about love? A marriage without love was unthinkable — and as for marrying the duke? Well, she didn't even like him very much.

He strolled across the room and folded his long length onto a similar chair on the other side of the fireplace.

She still hadn't responded to his unromantic suggestion. She took a deep breath and braced herself for his reaction. 'Your Grace, I will not be coerced into a marriage that I do not want. You have no wish to marry me — you could have the pick of the debutantes. Kindly find one of those to marry and leave me in peace.'

His eyes narrowed and his hands tightened on the arms of the chair but he didn't lose his temper. 'You are correct, Miss Richmond. Marrying you was not high on my list of priorities. However, I don't think you understand the position we find ourselves in. I know that you walked home but that does not alter the fact that my entire staff know you were there and that you arrived in a closed carriage with me. Servants are inveterate gossips — our indiscretion will be the talk of the neighbourhood by dinner tomorrow.'

'I believe you are forgetting the fact that you are a duke and therefore above any gossip or rumour. You may do as you wish and society will still hold you in good stead. Once everyone knows you are my legal guardian and have been since my father died, things will be as before.'

'It is not my reputation I am concerned about, my dear, but yours. Allow me to do the right thing by you and give you the protection of my name. I can assure you I have no wish to set up my nursery any time soon — you may continue to enjoy yourself, but do so at my expense.'

She yawned and was too late disguise it. It had been a very long day and she was too fatigued to argue the point with this formidable gentleman. She was sure Mama would agree with her — and she would not be obliged to marry him whatever he said to the contrary.

'I beg your pardon, sir, but I have no wish to continue this conversation. My answer remains the same.' She stood up and faced him. 'Admit it — if we could find a way out of this without damage to either of our reputations, you would be delighted.'

He joined her in front of the empty grate, reaching out to touch her cheek with his finger. 'Yes, you are correct. A reluctant bride is not something I had anticipated. Before you go, my dear, give me your word that you will agree to this union if circumstances force us to it.'

She was about to refuse outright, but then decided she would be safe enough agreeing, as she was certain there would be no unpleasant gossip and that her mother would support her. 'Very well, sir. I vow that I will marry you if I have no other choice.'

He nodded and half-smiled as if satisfied with her unenthusiastic answer. 'I shall depart the same way I came in. You must remain and secure the doors behind me. I shall be here tomorrow at noon. This matter will be decided then.'

He vanished into the darkness, leaving her thoughts in turmoil. Why was she so adamant she had no wish to marry him? He was a good deal older than her, but still in his prime — he was a handsome man and an entertaining companion when he cared to be. He was wealthy and possibly the only unmarried duke in the kingdom. He was right to castigate her. To marry a duke would be every debutante's dream, and yet she was refusing his offer. It made no sense. Why was she not overjoyed at the thought of being a duchess?

* * *

Aubrey recovered his horse on the shrubbery. 'Good grief! What the hell have you been eating, old fellow?' His mount's normally immaculate coat was liberally festooned with anonymous greenery. He pulled a large chunk from the animal's mouth and swung into the saddle.

He wasn't sure if he was dismayed or delighted that his proposal had been refused. He could see no way out of the impasse — was sure he would be obligated to honour his offer — but was prepared to wait and see how things developed in the morning.

Lydia was an intelligent girl, impeccably bred, reasonably attractive and young enough to learn how to become a suitable duchess. He swore under his breath; he should never have gone last night. He had attended the assembly under protest, but his sister was adamant they should put in an appearance. Margaret had said she wished to see Lydia amongst her friends as that way she would have a better opinion of the girl's behaviour in company.

His horse stumbled in the darkness and he lost a stirrup. He'd had sufficient disasters for one day and didn't want to add a fall to the list. Tomorrow was soon enough to worry about the future. His lips twitched. At least life would not be boring if he married Lydia Richmond.

The groom he had routed out of bed earlier was waiting to receive his horse.

He tossed the reins to the man, nodded his thanks and strode off to the house. The front door swung open as he reached the top of the steps. The footman bowed him in and the bolts were slammed across, the noise loud in the quiet house.

In his apartment his valet was waiting to help him disrobe. 'Wake me at my usual hour. I shall be riding to Ravenscroft after I have broken my fast.'

This would give him only a few hours' sleep, but it would have to do. He intended to get matters settled one way or the other before the day was out.

It did not occur to him that his manservant would also have little sleep, or that the footman and the groom would have to be up at dawn regardless of the time they had retired.

*　*　*

When Lydia finally arrived in the breakfast parlour the following morning, she was astonished to find her mother was not alone. Her uncle, Lord Richmond, had mysteriously arrived and was in the process of serving Mama with coddled eggs and slices of ham.

'Good morning, Lydia. I was beginning to think you were avoiding me,' Mama said without her customary smile.

Lydia thought it wise in the circumstances to curtsy to her uncle instead of just nodding in his direction. 'Good morning, Mama. Uncle Edward. I apologise if I am late, but I had no idea you were to be here so early today. We did not look forward to your visit until next week.'

He smiled and waved at the row of dishes on the sideboard. 'Sit down, my dear. Allow me to serve you your breakfast.' He placed the plate of food he had already dished up in front of Mama and then returned to the buffet. This gave Lydia time to be seated and try and assess the reason for the strained atmosphere.

'What would you like? A little of everything?'

'No, thank you, sir. I'm not especially hungry this morning — just some toasted bread, butter and conserve.' Whilst he was collecting this for her she poured herself a bowl of chocolate. Still Mama remained silent; this in itself was a rarity. Was this unnatural behaviour because of something she had done, or because of the unexpected arrival of her brother-in-law?

Her meagre breakfast was placed in front of her and her uncle returned to collect his own repast. This was the ideal time to question her mother. She lowered her voice. 'What is wrong? Why has Uncle Edward arrived before breakfast?'

'My dear, I can scarcely believe what he told me. He arrived at three o'clock in the morning to see the duke creeping around from the front of the house — '

'He has no right to comment on the duke's behaviour when arriving unannounced, in the middle of the night, himself.'

'That's as may be, Lydia, but he is

not an unmarried girl with a reputation to protect. How he behaves is his own business — how you behave is another matter.'

This entire conversation was conducted in a whisper but Lydia was fairly sure her uncle must be aware they were talking behind his back. He was not her guardian, had no say in her behaviour, and so she owed him no special treatment. She addressed his back. 'My lord, I am curious to know two things. One, why you chose to arrive unannounced in the middle of the night. Two, how you were able to recognise the duke without being seen yourself.'

He turned with an amiable smile, apparently unmoved by her outburst. Her mother, however, was extremely angry at her rudeness.

'I shall answer each question in turn. I should have been here during the afternoon, but one of my team lost a shoe and this delayed my journey by several hours. I had my coachman take me directly to the stable yard. On walking around to the front I could not fail to notice a massive stallion grazing in the shrubbery. I was curious as to the whereabouts of his owner, so walked around the house and could not help but see the gentleman in question conversing with you in the garden room. Neither could I help noticing that you were not appropriately attired.'

This information was obviously unknown to her mother, who threw down her cutlery in horror. 'How could you? What were you thinking of? Unless he is prepared to make you an offer, you are ruined.' She mopped her streaming cheeks before continuing. 'And more to the point, what was the duke doing here in the first place? I had no idea you and he were more than friends — '

This nonsense had gone on quite long enough. 'Mama, His Grace had come to see that I was safely home. I think that a perfectly reasonable action for my *legal guardian* to have taken. I am sorry that Lord Richmond considered it necessary to reveal this information in such a dramatic fashion. I believe this to be in the hope of creating a diversion and making his conduct seem less extraordinary.'

A charged silence filled the room. She hardly dared look up and meet the eyes of either her uncle or her mother. What had possessed her to say such things? It would appear that not only the duke and Lord Richmond were behaving out of character, but she too scarcely recognised herself as this outspoken young lady.

Eventually her mother spoke. 'Lydia, I am deeply shocked by your behaviour last night and this morning. I cannot imagine what has come over you. I believe His Grace might be right in saying Lady Alice is a bad influence.' Her uncle ignored them both, sat down, and began to eat his meal with evident relish.

She had lost what little appetite she

had arrived with. Carefully replacing her cutlery, she stood up and nodded to both adults. 'I beg pardon, but I'm feeling rather unwell. I'm going to walk in the garden until my digestion settles.'

Ignoring her mother's plea to return, Lydia ran through the house into the garden room and slid to a halt in front of the doors. Moments later she was running across the lawn, heading for the boathouse. No one would think to look for her there, as she had a horror of anything connected to open water. Although she disliked the lake, the boathouse was warm and comfortable: the perfect place to hide whilst she thought about what had happened over these past hours.

Inside, the water lapped the edge of the jetty; the rowing boat and punt were scarcely moving, encouraging her to step carefully down on to the polished surface of the punt. Her foot slipped and her heart almost jumped out of her chest, but she regained her balance and slid carefully onto the padded seat. The boat rocked alarmingly, splashing ice cold water into her lap, soaking her flimsy muslin gown.

'Botheration! How silly of me — now I shall be cold sitting here.' She spoke aloud, hoping the sound of her voice would make her feel less vulnerable and alone. She had made a sad mull of things. She had offended her guardian (she could still not quite grasp the fact that the duke held this position in her life), her dearest mama and Lord Richmond. She was in deep disgrace and could see no way to smooth matters over.

She settled on to the cushions, clutching nervously at the edge as the boat swayed unpleasantly, and reviewed the events of the past few hours. From whichever direction she came at the problem, it was perfectly clear to her with whom the blame lay. The duke had precipitated this disaster by deliberately tearing her gown and had then compounded his sin by demanding to come into the house in the middle of the night.

Why had he behaved in this extraordinary manner? She had known him for many years and not once had he shown the slightest inclination to levity or undisciplined actions. Indeed, one of his many faults was the fact that he rarely smiled and was in every way far too serious.

Another conundrum to solve was the fact that he had neglected to inform Mama or herself that he was in a position of authority over her. He had promised to explain his actions to her when he returned from the assembly last night, but she had absconded from his house and therefore the explanation had never been given.

Her eyes flickered shut. Despite the unpleasant proximity of the lake water, she was finding it quite peaceful stretched out in the punt. The sun was shining brightly through the glass in the roof and making the boathouse pleasantly warm. It would do no harm to doze for a while. No doubt her problems would seem less vexing when she awoke.

*   *   *

'Sinclair, what nonsense am I hearing from below stairs?' The strident voice of his sister jerked Aubrey from his rest in an armchair in his study. This was his sanctum. No one dared to disturb him here.

'What the devil do you mean by coming in here and shouting at me? I — '

'Listen to me, brother. There is the most scurrilous gossip circulating amongst the staff. I cannot believe what I am hearing. Is it possible that you did actually visit Miss Richmond in the middle of the night, and she received you?'

She had his undivided attention now. 'How the hell can you know that? We were not seen by any servants. For this information to have arrived here so soon meant someone must have been spying on us last night. Whoever it is has deliberately spread this gossip in order to ruin Miss Richmond.' He stood up, yawned and stretched. 'I went over to Ravenscroft to ensure that Miss Richmond was indeed at home safe and not wandering about in the woods. You will be relieved to know, Margaret, that I also proposed to her. Unfortunately, she turned me down — '

His sister stared at him as if he had run mad. 'Turned you down? You, the most eligible bachelor in the land, refused by a country miss? I cannot believe she would do such a thing.'

'You will be relieved to know that she promised she would accept my offer if there was the slightest risk to either of our reputations. Don't poker up at me, Margaret. This debacle is entirely my fault. The poor girl has no more desire to marry me than I do her.' His smile was sad as he continued. 'I believe she has her heart set on a romantic union with a dashing young cavalry officer. I must get over to Ravenscroft immediately, speak to Lady Richmond and make our betrothal official.' He turned to leave but his sister called him back.

'Sinclair, you cannot go as you are. You are as bearded as a pirate — your hair is standing on end and your topcoat looks as though you have been sleeping in it.'

He laughed. 'That is because I have been doing exactly that. Don't fret, I shall get myself shaved and change my raiment before I go. Please don't look so dejected, my dear. This is not a complete disaster. Lydia Richmond will make me a perfectly good wife.'

6

A loud voice calling her name dragged Lydia from a deep sleep. She shot upright, quite forgetting she was lying in a punt. The boat rocked violently and she was catapulted over the side into the murky water of the boathouse. The icy water shocked her awake. She couldn't swim. She was going to drown and nobody knew where she was. Frantically she clawed at the side of the boat, screaming for help as the weight of her sodden gown began to pull her to the bottom of the lake.

As she sank she closed her eyes and prayed to the Almighty that someone might arrive in time and save her from a horrible death. Then somebody reached in and grabbed her flailing arms and she was heaved upright.

'You can stand; the water is only waist-deep in here. Don't panic —

you're perfectly safe.' The duke was leaning over the side of the punt, grinning at her.

She was wet, cold, and he had the temerity to laugh at her. Indignation replaced her fear. 'Do you intend to leave me here, or are you going to assist me out of the water?' Not giving him time to answer, she launched herself forward and clutched his lapels. She caught him unawares and he was unable to stop himself somersaulting into the water beside her.

The resulting splash as he submerged engulfed her. For the second time she sank to the bottom, swallowing what felt like several pints of dirty water on the way down. The duke recovered his feet and grabbed Lydia under the arms and shoved her none too gently into the punt, where she lay coughing and spluttering and unable to move.

'For God's sake, what the hell do you think you are doing, you stupid girl? Were you trying to drown us both?' This was shouted into her ear and had the desired effect. She rolled over and pushed herself onto her knees.

'I wish I had drowned you. Then I would not have to marry you.'

He waded to the side and scrambled out, to stand dripping and seething at the side of the punt. His exit had sent the boat wildly rocking again. If she went into the lake again she would truly kill him.

'Believe me, young lady, if there was any way I could avoid tying myself to you I would take it. You are, without doubt, the most irritating and insolent girl it has ever been my misfortune to meet.' His tirade was somewhat spoilt by the fact that he was dripping wet.

Whilst he was choking and swearing in a most ungentlemanly manner, she took the opportunity to step from the punt and run out of the boathouse. She had lost both her slippers, her pretty gown was quite ruined and her hair hung in a bedraggled and unattractive fashion around her shoulders. At the door she glanced back to see him leaning against the wall, attempting to empty the water from his once immaculate Hessians. His cravat was an interesting shade of green, his topcoat ripped at the seams; and as for his calfskin unmentionables — they clung to him like a second skin.

Her eyes rounded in shock. With fiery cheeks she fled for the safety of the house, trying to blot out what she had just seen. She raced through the garden and around to the side door that should give her the opportunity to reach her own apartment without being seen in such disarray.

Her maid greeted her appearance with a screech of horror. 'Miss Richmond, whatever next! Did you fall into the lake?'

'His Grace is in a worse state than I am. I do believe his smart clothes are all quite beyond repair.' Some imp of mischief made her rush to the window in order to watch his progress across the grass. He had removed his topcoat, untucked his shirt so that it hung in concealing folds around his skin-tight breeches, and was carrying his boots in one hand. He had been reduced from a high-and-mighty aristocrat to a sorry specimen indeed. A bubble of mirth rose in her throat and she laughed out loud. He, at that precise moment, stopped and looked up at her window.

All desire to laugh shrivelled under his arctic stare. She stepped backwards, away from the window, knowing she had turned a bad situation into a disaster. How could she marry a man who hated her? Her stomach rebelled and she cast up her accounts onto the polished floorboards, the humiliation just adding to her distress.

She was emerging from her bath when her mother rushed into her bedchamber. 'Lydia, whatever possessed you to push His Grace into the lake? Your uncle was unable to placate him and he has departed in high dudgeon.'

Enveloped in a giant bath sheet, warm at last, Lydia was able to smile ruefully at the charges. 'Actually, Mama, I fell in, and whilst he was attempting to pull me out I inadvertently pulled him in. I can promise you it was not deliberate. I cannot tell you how sorry I am that my clumsiness caused him to get wet.'

The towel trailed behind her as she slipped behind the screen in order to pull on her nightgown and wrapper. She had no intention of going downstairs again today just in case the duke decided to come back for a reckoning.

'Well, my love, all I can say is that you have not endeared yourself to him. I have never seen a man so enraged. This does not bode well for your future happiness.'

Lydia felt as if she had plunged headfirst into the icy water of the lake for a second time. She shuddered and all but collapsed. Immediately Jenny and her mother were at her side offering support and comfort. She was escorted to her bed and she didn't protest. Mama promised to return to see how she did later and Jenny was dispatched to the kitchen to fetch a bowl of broth and some tea.

The last thing she wanted was to eat, but she hadn't the heart to say no when both her maid and her mother were being so kind. She sank into the pillows and closed her eyes. An image of the duke's chiselled features, his expression harsh, filled her head. Mama was right — to marry him without true love would have been difficult, but a union with the gentleman who held her in dislike would be a nightmare.

When Jenny returned Lydia pretended to be asleep. She hid her head beneath the covers until the room was silent again. The girl had closed the shutters and the chamber was dark. Lydia was awake most of the night trying to think of a way to avoid embarking on a loveless marriage; she was no nearer a solution when she eventually fell asleep just before dawn.

★　★　★

When Aubrey slid off the saddle for the second time he decided he might be better off walking — that was, if his boots were not too sodden to be wearable. Whilst he was regaining his seat his stallion ambled into the hedgerow and began to graze on the brambles. Riding in bare feet was not a pleasant experience and neither was slithering all over the place because his breeches were slimy with mud.

He had discarded his ruined topcoat and cravat and was tempted to do the same with his shirt. The fine cotton was transparent when wet, so he might just as well be riding without it. He was about to pull it over his head when he reconsidered. His sister would be scandalised to see him as he was, God knew what she would do if he arrived at Stenning semi-naked.

When he'd fallen headlong into the lake he had been annoyed with Miss Richmond for her part in his misfortune, but seeing her laughing at him from her bedroom window had sent a surge of rage around his body, so fierce that if he had been able to lay hands on her he might well have strangled her.

God's teeth! What was he thinking? He had laughed at her as she stood dripping and dishevelled up to her waist in the murky water. She was right to find him a figure of fun and he was an idiot to have been so angry. His mouth curved. The poor girl must have been as embarrassed and humiliated as he was. 'Come along, Brutus. You have done enough munching for one day. We must get back. I need a bath and a change of raiment and then I shall have to return and attempt to mend some fences with my future wife.'

The horse flicked his ears as if listening to him. By the time Aubrey arrived at Stenning his good humour was restored and he was almost beginning to consider the incident as an amusing experience. Unfortunately, his sister thought differently. He handed his horse to a groom and strolled around to the front door. Perhaps it would have been better to enter via a less conspicuous route — but he was the lord and master here and felt no need to creep about his own house. He was greeted by a noise that would have not been out of place at Billingsgate fish market.

'Sinclair, have you taken leave of your senses? To be parading around the countryside as you are is beyond belief. You will be the talk of the neighbourhood.' Margaret drew breath to continue her tirade. He raised his hand and shook his head.

'Thank you, sister. I'm well aware of my dilapidation. However, as I own most of the village and its environs, I hardly think my tenants are about to comment. Remember, my dear, that I am the Duke of Stenning and therefore can do as I wish without fear of criticism or censure.' With a casual wave in her direction he strolled past and bounded up the stairs, where his valet was already drawing water for his bath. He smiled as he disrobed. It never failed to amaze him how rapidly word spread through his vast establishment.

After his ablutions he selected a fresh outfit and a new pair of boots, and was ready to return to Ravenscroft. He had to make another offer to Miss Richmond. He chuckled and his man was so startled by this unusual occurrence that he dropped the armful of wet towels he was removing from the bathing room. Being married to this young lady would not be boring — no doubt she would stagger from one disaster to another and involve him in all of them.

One of the reasons he had never fallen into the parson's mouse trap was because he had found every young lady that had been thrust under his nose by matchmaking mamas insipid and without wit or sparkle. For all her faults — and they were legion — Lydia Richmond was as different from those simpering debutantes as chalk was to cheese. She was lively, intelligent, and the only person of his acquaintance who had ever dared to insult him. Yes, maybe this union would not be quite such a disaster. But first he must convince the lady in question that she had no option but to become his duchess.

When he arrived downstairs he found his entire family waiting for him. By the time he had explained how he came to return drenched to the skin it was too late to ride over to Ravenscroft. He spent an hour in the billiard room with his brothers and brother-in-law before returning to his apartment to change for the third time that day, into his evening rig.

★ ★ ★

Lydia was already dressed when her abigail arrived with her morning chocolate. 'Jenny, as you can see, I am going riding. Thank you for bringing me my drink, but I do not require it today. Please, do not let it go to waste.'

'What shall I put out for you, Miss Richmond?'

'Anything — whatever you like — I know I can rely on your good taste. I shall not be above two hours, so expect me back at nine o'clock. I shall not require a bath; a wash will be sufficient.'

Downstairs the house was silent. Her mother rarely rose before noon and she had no idea at what time Lord Richmond would appear, but doubted he would bother to rise from his bed any earlier than Mama. Therefore she had ample time for her ride before having to face them. She refused to contemplate her forthcoming meeting with the duke; he would not come until the afternoon.

Her mount, a pretty dapple grey mare called Storm, was already tacked and waiting for her. A groom tossed her into the saddle and then scrambled aboard a solid bay gelding in order to accompany her.

'I intend to ride to the coast, Patrick. The tide is low this morning and we can gallop along the beach.'

He touched his forelock and nodded.

'Yes, Miss Richmond. It's a grand day, to be sure, for riding along the sand.'

She returned his smile. There was something about this flame-haired Irishman that appealed to her. Where Thomas, the head groom, had discovered him she had no idea, but he was an attractive addition to the outside staff. She always asked him when she rode out.

The wind was brisk and had a nip of autumn in it. Both horses were skittish and she was relieved they arrived at the beach without mishap. A mile or more of hard, wet sand stretched in front of her and she settled into the saddle and gave Storm her head. The wild gallop was just what she needed — it cleared her head and she reined in at the far end of the sand feeling more sanguine about her forthcoming appointment with the duke.

She guided the mare up the steep, sandy path that led to the grassy headland which ran along the coast. At the top she turned in the saddle and spoke to Patrick. 'We will return through the village as I wish to call in and speak to the Lady Alice.'

Her friend lived just outside Stenning in a substantial manor house. Although ridiculously early, she was certain Alice would be up and eager to see her. She had so much to tell her since the assembly. She could hardly credit the extraordinary events that had taken place over the past two days. No doubt there would also be gossip to hear about the ball. She wondered if Alice had managed to dance with as many officers as she'd planned to.

Sure enough, her friend was indeed happy to see her. She had seen Lydia trotting down the drive and was waiting on the front porch when she arrived. 'I cannot tell you how delighted I am to see you. You will not believe what I have to tell you. I have asked for breakfast to be served early as I know that you are always ready to eat.' Alice wrinkled her nose as Lydia embraced her. 'Let us hope we do not encounter Mama. She would be scandalised to find you reeking of the stable in her breakfast parlour.'

'You know me so well. I am famished. I cannot believe what you have to impart will be as momentous as my news. However, shall we eat before we talk?'

Half an hour later Lydia had eaten her fill. Alice had barely touched her plate and was fidgeting in her chair. 'Shall we go up to your chambers?' Lydia suggested. 'If we remain here we risk being interrupted.'

'Yes. Oh do hurry up; you have been an age. I cannot understand why you remain so slender when you consume as much as a gardener.'

Giggling together, they ran up the main staircase and into the security of Alice's elegant apartment. Lydia curled up in her favourite chair and waited expectantly to hear the news. 'Well, what has happened to you that is making you so agitated?' Her news must wait until her friend had unburdened herself.

'After you tore your gown and had to go home, I met the man that I intend to marry.'

Whatever Lydia had expected, it had not been this. 'What do you mean? Who did you meet? How can you possibly know he is the man you wish to spend the rest of your life with?'

'His name is Captain Adam Duvall. He's the youngest son of the Earl of Devonport. He has a small estate of his own, inherited from a distant relative, and is the most handsome, adorable, wonderful man you could ever hope to meet.'

'You cannot possibly be in love with him after one meeting. It is an infatuation. No one can be sure they have met the man of their dreams so soon.'

Alice clasped her hands to her bosom like the heroine in one of the Gothic novels she was addicted to. 'We danced only twice, but we managed to spend time together at supper. We met yesterday at the beach and I cannot describe to you how it felt to be with him.'

Lydia had a bad feeling about this. 'Please tell me that you were not unaccompanied? You did not dismount?'

Her friend blushed and wouldn't meet her look. 'He is a gentleman. He said he loved me, and that I was an angel come to save him. He said he would speak to Papa, but not until we have had the opportunity to spend time together at another function. There is to be a social evening at the Lawsons' tomorrow night and we are to attend. I do hope you will be there too. I wish you to meet him.'

'I'm not sure if I can come. Lord Richmond has arrived unexpectedly and I fear my time might no longer be my own. I, too, have extraordinary news for you.' She took a deep breath and launched into her own unbelievable tale. When she had completed it Alice's reaction was completely unexpected.

'How exciting! We shall both be

married before Christmas — you a duchess and I a soldier's wife. And to think only the other day we were quite certain that we would remain single until we were one-and-twenty.'

7

The ride from the village to Ravenscroft scarcely gave Lydia time to process what Alice had told her. For her friend to believe herself in love after so short a time was possible, as she was of a romantic nature — however, it was hardly credible that a military man should be similarly afflicted. Captain Duvall, according to Alice, was a gentleman of means and therefore had no need to search out a rich heiress. Even so, Lydia decided she owed it to her bosom friend to investigate this young man before there was no alternative but a hasty marriage.

She clattered into the stable yard and a young groom rushed forward to take the mare. Before she could dismount the duke appeared through the arch that led to the house and strode up to her.

'Good morning, my dear. Did you enjoy your ride?'

Bemused at his genial enquiry, she half-smiled and nodded. 'Yes, thank you, Your Grace; most enjoyable. I apologise for my absence, but I did not expect you to call before breakfast.' She wished her comment unspoken but his jaw hardened and he looked less friendly.

'Obviously not; however, we have pressing matters to decide, and the sooner the better.' He stepped up to Storm and without a by-your-leave snatched her from the saddle. He then threaded her gloved hand through his arm and she had no option but to trail along beside him like a recalcitrant child.

This would not do. If she was old enough to be his wife then she should be treated as an adult and not dragged about the place like this. She dug in her heels, forcing him to halt. 'Your Grace, kindly release my arm. I am quite capable of walking to my own house without your assistance.'

'Indeed you are, Miss Richmond, but you also have an alarming tendency to run away when thwarted.' He stared down his aristocratic nose at her and she stared back.

This was a pivotal moment in their relationship. If she did not wish to be permanently subservient to this intimidating man, then she must stand her ground. Her hands were clenched and if her back had not been supported against the hedge, she feared she might collapse in a heap at his feet. He removed his fingers from around her arm and she was free. He was correct — her first instinct was to turn tail and run. But something held her firm and she rubbed her arm where his fingers had been gripping as if he had hurt her.

Instantly his expression changed to concern. 'I hurt you — I am a brute and I apologise unreservedly. I — '

For a second she was tempted to let him squirm. 'Please, Your Grace. You have no need to apologise. I was being deliberately provocative. Your hold was gentle,' she grinned at him, 'but exceedingly firm.'

'You are a minx, my dear girl, and I can see I shall have to be vigilant if I do not wish to be bested on every occasion.' He nodded and, with a twinkle in his eye, held out his arm. 'Miss Richmond, would you allow me the honour of escorting you inside?'

She nodded regally. 'Thank you, Your Grace. I should be delighted to accept your kind offer.' The words hung in the air between them and the atmosphere changed. She dropped her hand and pressed herself into the hedge.

'God dammit to hell! This is not how it should be. But let us get this wretched business out of the way and then we can behave sensibly again.' He drew himself up to his full height and bowed deeply. He did not drop to one knee again. 'Miss Richmond, I am asking you for a second time if you will kindly make me the happiest of men and accept my proposal. Will you be my bride?'

She wanted to scream no — every instinct told her the union between them would be an unmitigated disaster — but she nodded. She was unable to speak the words, but he appeared satisfied with her half-hearted response.

'Excellent. My sister can organise this event for us. I trust that the announcement will be sufficient to silence the gossip. I have already spoken to Lady Richmond and she is of the same opinion as I — there is no need to delay our nuptials. The banns will be read as soon as can be arranged and we will be married next month.'

This finally roused Lydia. 'What about my bride clothes? Surely I will be allowed time to have those made?'

'Your mama has assured me your wardrobe is more than adequate. We shall go to London in the new year and you can order whatever you like for the coming season.'

She blinked away her tears. There was no point in arguing; his mind was made up. And her mother, for some unknown reason, had abandoned her to her fate. 'Very well, Your Grace. Next month it shall be.' She moved away from the protection of the foliage and stepped around him as if he were dangerous to touch. 'In which case, Your Grace, I see no need for you to accompany me further. No doubt you have more important business to attend to, so I bid you good morning.'

He raised his hand to restrain her, then let it fall. 'My dear, I wish things were as simple as that. Shall we take a turn around the garden?'

She could hardly refuse when he asked her so politely. 'Very well. I think I should prefer to talk outside.' Should she explain why she was so reluctant to go into the house with him?

'We can be uninterrupted out here; this conversation is nobody's business but ours.'

He didn't offer his arm but stepped aside, allowing her to lead the way. Neither of them spoke until they were safely away from the house. She wasn't sure in which direction to go and hesitated.

'Shall we sit here, in this rose arbour? Or do you wish to wander about the garden, Your Grace?'

'This will do perfectly. No, don't sit yet — let me remove the debris.' He busied himself sweeping away the accumulation of leaves and bird droppings. She was surprised he felt no repugnance — after all he was not wearing gloves.

As they were both wearing riding clothes, sitting on the marble bench would not have been a problem for either of them. Was he as nervous as she about the forthcoming discussion? This thought gave her confidence and she was able to smile her thanks before settling down in the far corner of the arbour, leaving him ample room to be seated without the necessity of touching her.

'What else is there to discuss?' She hadn't meant to sound so abrupt.

He frowned. 'I need to make it clear

to you that I have no intention of sharing your bed. You are scarcely out of the school room after all, and I have no need of an heir.'

His bald statement shocked her to the core. As always she spoke without artifice, equally straightforward. 'I cannot believe you wish to deny me the one compensation for marrying a man I do not love. Having children is the only thing that will make this arrangement bearable.'

He rubbed his hand across his eyes and sighed. If she didn't know better she would think he looked defeated. He straightened and looked her straight in the eye. 'I did not say I would never set up my nursery, just that I have no intention of making love to someone as young as you.'

Heat spread from her toes to her crown, but she did not look away. He was offering her a marriage in name only, so why did she not jump at the chance? 'I am not a child, Your Grace. I am a grown woman and if I am considered old enough to say my vows next month, then I'm old enough to be the mother of your children.'

For a moment nothing happened, then he reached out and slid his arms around her waist. Before she could protest she was on his lap. Her hand pressed against his chest — his heart hammered beneath her fingers. His eyes had darkened and a dark flush ran along his cheekbones. He bent his head until his mouth was brushing her ear. 'Well, sweetheart, let us discover just how grown-up you are.'

The heat off his breath sent tremors around her body. There was an unpleasant hardness beneath her bottom. She had unleashed something she could not control. His right hand was cupping her breast and with his left he tilted her chin. She closed her eyes, unable to look at him anymore. His mouth closed over hers, his lips hard and demanding. She had never experienced anything so unpleasant, and then it got worse. His tongue forced its way between her parted lips.

This intrusion was too much. She bit down and tasted the salty tang of his blood. His grip loosened and she was free. She didn't wait on him to call her back but raced as if the devil was at her heels to the security of the house.

★   ★   ★

Aubrey spat out the blood from his mouth and wiped his lips on his sleeve. He had not intended to take matters so far, merely scare Lydia and make her revoke her demand that they share a bed. Instead he had revolted her, possibly given her a fear of intimacy. Something had happened to him when she was in his arms. His ardour had been aroused, he had forgotten she was little more than a school room miss, and kissed her as if she was in love with him.

He had made a difficult situation impossible. There was little point in chasing after her; she would already be hiding in her apartment. He didn't blame her this time for running away. He wiped a second dribble of blood from his chin and smiled ruefully. She had done exactly the right thing. He had always considered himself a man of sense, of understanding, but today he had behaved like the veriest greenhorn. He should have known immediately she had no idea what took place between a man and a woman when conceiving a child.

He decided it would be better if he only met her in public until they were married. They had the rest of their lives to get to know each other, so why risk alienating her further? Margaret must begin the organisation of the wedding whilst he sent his man of affairs to speak to the rector.

His visit to Ravenscroft had been considerably shorter than he had anticipated. His intention had been to speak to Lady Richmond about financial matters, but this would have to wait until a more opportune time. He was greeted by his sister as he strolled into the drawing-room.

'Sinclair, there you are. Have you spoken to Miss Richmond and made your engagement official?'

'I have. We are to be married next month, so I am relying on you to be able to organise everything in time.'

'Are you quite mad? To marry in such haste will give rise to even more gossip — everyone will think Miss Richmond is in an interesting condition. Surely Lady Richmond did not agree to this?'

'I was unable to speak to her this morning. I can see no reason to delay.' He grinned and gave his most superior stare. 'As I have told you before, sister, I am a duke and can do no wrong. Only lesser mortals need worry about such things.'

'You are quite impossible. I am at a loss to understand why you are in such a hurry to tie the knot when, in the circumstances, a long engagement might be beneficial for both of you.'

'What circumstances are these?' His enquiry was silky smooth, but his sister heeded the warning.

'Miss Richmond is very young and, although you have known her for several years, I doubt that she has ever viewed you as a possible husband. You can be charming when you choose to be — why not spend a few weeks at least courting her before dragging her up the aisle? You have stopped the gossip by announcing your betrothal. I'm sure nobody expects you to be married with such indecent haste.'

He frowned. Why did he wish his marriage to take place as soon? It made no sense. Margaret was quite correct: it would be far better to spend time wooing his future bride. He was about to agree when something astounding rocked him back on his heels.

His desire to tie the knot so speedily was because he feared Lydia would find a way to break the engagement if he did not. Suddenly his extraordinary behaviour over the past two days made sense.

He was in love with her. Her announcement that she had no intention of marrying before she was one-and-twenty, and that when she did it would be to an officer, had set things in motion. He had, without realising it, deliberately compromised her so she would not be lost to him.

Margaret was staring at him as if he had lost his senses. 'Are you quite well? You look decidedly strange.'

He laughed out loud. 'I have never been better. I thought I was losing my mind, but now everything is clear to me. You are quite right, sister. I should allow Miss Richmond time to adjust, but I have no intention of doing so. Therefore, will you please arrange for the wedding breakfast and a celebratory ball to follow that evening? Just close friends and family at the ceremony and breakfast, but invite everyone to the ball. I shall get my man of affairs to arrange some sort of event to mark the occasion for the tenants and villagers. The ceremony will be four weeks from today — the banns will have been read and arrangements made by then. Pray forgive me, but I have business to attend to.' He turned to go and then remembered something else. 'We will be going to the Lawsons' musicale tomorrow night.'

★　★　★

Lydia had recovered her composure by the time she reached the side door. He was quite correct; she did have a tendency to bolt when things went wrong. No wonder he thought her a child.

There were several things she needed to do and the first of these was speak to her mother. Although it was nearly ten o'clock, no one was about. She would go to her mother's apartment — what she had to say could not wait a moment longer. There were voices coming from the parlour so she could be sure her mother was dressed. She knocked on the door and was invited to enter.

'My darling girl, is everything settled? Did the duke propose?'

'Yes, Mama, he did. We are to be married next month. I am at a loss to understand why he believes we must be wed so soon.'

Her mother, who was sitting on the chaise-longue drinking her morning chocolate, patted the empty space beside her. 'Sit down, my love. There are things we need to talk about.' When Lydia was settled she smiled fondly at her. 'For some time now I have suspected that the duke has developed feelings for you. Why else did he come to visit so regularly?'

'You forget that he is my guardian — he came for that reason only. He no more has feelings for me than I do for him. This will be an arranged marriage, and we will both have to make the best of it.'

'I shall not argue the point, my dear. The important thing is that you will be his duchess. This must be the fulfilment of all your dreams. I know you said you would marry no one until you were of age, and that you had the fancy to be a wife of an officer, but that is the talk of a romantic child. You will be a leader of fashion, a society hostess, mix in the highest echelons — what more could you want?'

'I want to be in love with my husband and for him to feel the same way about me. It doesn't matter if one is a duchess or a commoner — what is important is to be marrying for love.'

Her mother sipped her chocolate thoughtfully. 'What is it that you object to about your future husband? He is in his prime, a handsome man, intelligent, witty, and kind to his servants and animals. He is also one of the warmest men in England. I suggest that you forget your foolishness and start counting your blessings.'

'He may be all those things, but is also dictatorial, arrogant and quick-tempered. Anyway, I have agreed to marry him so I might as well stop bemoaning the fact that there is no love between us and look forward to living in the lap of luxury.' She smiled. 'After all, better to be a miserable duchess than a happy pauper.'

'Don't be ridiculous, child. I don't know what's come over you these past few days. Now, I expect you are eager to know why Lord Richmond has arrived so early.'

'I am. I had come here especially to ask you exactly that.'

Her mother fiddled with her gown, an unbecoming flush staining her cheeks. 'There is something you should know. Your uncle and your papa were estranged because of me. I was in love with your uncle but my parents wished me to marry your father. As a dutiful daughter I did as I was bid — and I am happy to tell you that love grew over the years and I was very happy.'

Lydia finally understood why her father and his brother had been estranged. 'How old were you?'

'I was seventeen, and you were born

two weeks before my eighteenth birthday. It was your arrival that brought us
together.'

'I am glad you were both happy, but
what about my uncle? Has he come to
make you an offer? Is that why you are
so eager for me to leave?'

8

Lady Richmond jumped to her feet and her half-empty bowl of chocolate flew into Lydia's lap. 'How can you say such things? You are my daughter. I would never do anything detrimental to your happiness. I did not ask him to come here — I can send him away, if that's what you would prefer.'

Lydia mopped ineffectually at the puddle of brown liquid. 'Please forgive me. I spoke without thinking. I thought you would support me in my wish to avoid this marriage; that you understood how I felt. I understand now how things are. This is exactly the sort of match any mama would dream of for their daughter.' She stood up and embraced her mother. 'I am fortunate that someone as illustrious as the Duke of Stenning wishes to marry me, even though he would not have offered unless obliged to. From this moment I shall be content and promise I will be the best wife I can.'

'When you have your first baby, everything will fall into place as it did for me.'

Was this the time to tell her mother how things had ended between her and the duke? That her suggestion they consummate the marriage had caused him to behave in an ungentlemanly fashion, and his advances had been quite repellent? She had a vague idea what took place in the marriage bed in order to produce a baby, so after her experience this morning she would make sure she remained a maiden as long as possible.

'I am sure that it will, Mama. I am going to look through my wardrobe and check that I have everything I need. His Grace insists that I see a London modiste when we go up for the season next year. All I really want to know is if I have something suitable for a wedding dress.'

'Darling girl, there is nothing I should like to do more than help you, but unfortunately I am engaged for the rest of the day. I have quite ruined your habit, so that is one thing that needs to go on your list. Why not send a note to Lady Alice and ask her to help you?'

Only as she stripped off her stained skirt did Lydia realise her mother had not answered the question about Lord Richmond's proposal. She shrugged. Worrying about her mother's future plans was pointless — she had her own wedding to get through first. For all her brave words, she was not eagerly anticipating becoming a duchess or being a society hostess. In fact, she had no inclination at all to become anyone's wife — especially not the duke, who was too old and set in his ways to make someone her age a satisfactory husband.

A footman was sent the village with a note for Alice, and the reply was that she was to expect her friend by noon. She would have luncheon sent up to her, thus avoiding any necessity to be downstairs. She was on tenterhooks all morning expecting the duke to arrive and insist on speaking to her.

* * *

Alice had her maid with her. The girl staggered in under an arm full of gowns. 'Look what I have brought for you, Lydia. I'm sure between us we can find something suitable for your wedding day.' She gestured to her abigail and the clothes were dropped onto the chaise longue.

'How kind of you, Alice. Jenny is putting out anything she thinks might do. Perhaps Sally can do the same with your gowns? They could be draped across the back of the day bed.'

Whilst this was being done, Lydia led the way into her bed chamber. 'I had no idea I owned so many pretty gowns.' She held each one in turn for her friend to comment on, but none of them came up to scratch. 'Oh dear! Are we being too particular? Maybe the pink silk with the roses around the neckline and hem would do — I have a matching bonnet, gloves and slippers.'

'Shall we look at what I brought over? Unfortunately our feet are not the same size, so even though there are slippers that accompany each ensemble, they will not do. There are half-a-dozen bonnets in the carriage. If you decide on one of these gowns then I shall send Sally to fetch the appropriate one.'

The cascade of colour on the day bed was in sharp contrast to the pastel shades of Lydia's own dresses. Alice's garments reflected her lively personality and the fact that her mother was over-indulgent. Young ladies were not expected to wear bright colours, but her friend ignored this rule and had cerise, peacock-blue, gold and emerald-green ensembles. The gowns were made of silk, Indian cotton, muslin and tulle.

'The duke will expect me to wear something demure, something in keeping with his status. However, I think I shall surprise him. How fortunate that we can share our gowns; although I cannot remember more than one occasion when you have borrowed anything from me.'

Alice ran across and snatched up the emerald-green silk. 'This would be perfect for you, as it exactly matches the colour of your eyes.' She flapped it and the fine tulle separated from the silk petticoat, revealing that the bright colour came from the undergarment and not the overskirt.

'If the petticoat could be replaced with something less startling, then I think this would be perfect. Do you have something in gold that would work?'

Sally rummaged through the gowns and carefully removed the golden petticoat from a different ensemble and swapped it with the emerald green.

'I shall try it on, but first Jenny must rearrange my hair. Can the bonnet be fetched? I would like to see both the gold and green.'

In less than an hour Lydia was dressed in the borrowed finery, her hair in a chignon which allowed the pretty gold silk-lined bonnet to fit. Slowly, she rotated in front of the full-length glass. For once Alice was silent.

'You look so beautiful, like a princess from a fairy tale. I much prefer this gown with the gold. The emerald overskirt is now less . . . '

'Less startling?' Lydia giggled and clapped her hands. 'Jenny, please hide this ensemble where it can't be seen. I have no wish for anyone else to know what I'm going to wear on my wedding day.' They were all aware the only person she didn't wish to see her choice was her mama. 'I think I shall have my cream striped muslin with the silk underskirt set out. If Lady Richmond enquires, kindly show her that.'

'Are you coming to the musicale tonight? I do so want to introduce you to Captain Duvall.'

'I haven't spoken to Mama, but I can see no reason why we should not come.

Of course, if the duke sends word that I accompany him elsewhere, then I suppose I must do as he bids.'

'It is now well past the accepted time for morning calls — I wonder why he hasn't come to see you? Anyway, I must return home. I wish to have ample time to prepare for this evening's outing.'

After Alice had gone, Lydia curled up in the window seat to read. She was immersed in her book and didn't hear her parlour door open. When the duke cleared his throat he was standing no more than a yard from her. His unexpected appearance made her heart skitter and her book fall unnoticed to the floor.

'Your Grace, what are you doing here? Why did no one announce you?'

'I beg your pardon, Miss Richmond, but Lady Richmond told me to announce myself. I knocked, but you failed to hear.' He reached down and picked up the book. He examined the interior and smiled in that superior fashion of his. 'As to why I am here, my dear, there are still many matters we have to discuss.' He waved at a chair and raised an eyebrow. She nodded, and he sat. 'It would appear, according to my sister, that you should be consulted about the arrangements for our nuptials.' He didn't sound as if he were convinced by his sister's advice.

She swung her legs to the floor. 'It is a matter of indifference to me. I have agreed to marry you; is it part of the agreement that I pretend enthusiasm too?' How unpleasant she sounded — why did he bring out the very worst in her?

'Very well, I shall tell you what is to happen and I do not require that you express an opinion. We shall be married in the Stenning family chapel at eleven o'clock on the third Saturday of November. There will be a wedding breakfast for close family and a celebration ball for friends and neighbours — '

Forgetting she was supposed to remain silent, Lydia burst out, 'You cannot have a ball — Lady Alice has already sent out invitations for her anniversary ball to be held on the following Saturday.'

Instead of being annoyed by her interruption, he struck his forehead and said a most unsuitable word. 'Dammit! I have the card — how could I have forgotten? So, if we are not to have a celebration ball, what shall we do instead? There is to be no wedding trip, as travelling in December can be difficult and unpleasant. I thought we might visit the lakes next summer.'

'I would much prefer it if we did nothing at all. A small family ceremony would be perfect. We can attend Lady Alice's ball and everyone will have the opportunity to congratulate us then. Perhaps we could do something for the new year instead?'

He nodded and stretched out his booted legs. How very long they were; she could not help but notice the firmness of his thighs. Blushing furiously, she fiddled with her sash until she had regained her composure.

'There is something I must insist on, my dear. For us to come out with our reputations unscathed it must appear this is a love match. Why else would we marry in such a rush?'

She was about to argue that they both disliked each other and such a pretence would be impossible, when she reconsidered. She closed her eyes and took several deep breaths. 'That is an excellent idea, sir, and what better place to do it than at the ball?' She smiled at him and his eyes danced. 'Unfortunately, play-acting has never been a strength of mine. Are you an accomplished thespian?'

He clutched his chest and rolled his eyes before fixing the most idiotic expression on his face. 'My darling, I adore you. You are an angel sent from heaven to make me happy.'

She choked and was unable to restrain her giggles. 'And you, sir, are quite ridiculous. If *you* behave like a simpleton then I will not be answerable for my actions.'

He chuckled and the atmosphere lightened. 'Doing it rather too brown, do you think? Don't worry, sweetheart; I promise you the evening will be a success for both of us.' He stood up and offered her his hand. It would seem churlish to refuse this gesture of friendship. His fingers closed around hers and he gently pulled her to her feet, but immediately released his grip.

'Is there anything else we need to discuss, Your Grace?'

He grinned. 'I suppose it is too much to ask that you call me by my given name?'

'Indeed it is. It would be most irregular.' She tilted her head to one side as if considering her answer. 'However, I am prepared to compromise and call you either Stenning or Sinclair — which would you prefer?'

'I'd prefer that you called me Aubrey, but we'll settle for Sinclair.' He half-bowed before adding, 'I shall call you Lydia in future, for I cannot abide the idea of referring to you as anything else.' He reached into his waistcoat pocket and produced a small square box. 'You must wear this in future. It is a family heirloom.' He tossed it casually in her direction and she caught it with one hand. Hardly a romantic gesture! He prepared to leave, obviously satisfied with the outcome of his visit.

'I am going to the musicale at the Lawsons' tonight — shall I see you there?' she asked him.

He paused at the door and shook his head slightly. 'No, Lydia, you will not see me *there* . . . ' She couldn't stop the relief showing on her face. 'I am sorry to disappoint you, but I shall be collecting you in my carriage at precisely seven o'clock.'

The door closed softly behind him. She was not sure if she was angry because he had come out best again, or excited at the thought of another sparring match with her future husband. She returned to the window seat in order to watch him ride away on his bay stallion. Halfway down the drive he circled his mount and raised his hand in her direction. How could he have known she would be watching him? She was tempted to ignore this gesture, but then a quite different approach occurred to her.

She knelt on the seat and waved gaily. He tipped his hat and continued his journey. He had said they must pretend to be in love. She was fairly sure he had meant this charade to begin after their wedding, but he was going to get a surprise this evening. She intended to play the part of a besotted young lady to perfection. She could hardly wait to see his face when she fawned over him in public.

* * *

Aubrey arrived home in a better frame of mind than he had left. Lydia, if not exactly eager to marry him, now seemed less reluctant. He would stick to his word and stay away from her bed, but the more time he spent with her, the harder this was going to be. He must be very careful not to frighten her as he had done this morning. He would gently court her until she came to him. He sincerely hoped he could persuade her to fall in love with him sooner rather than later.

Margaret greeted him with affection. 'That is excellent news, Sinclair. You can be an extremely persuasive and charming gentleman when you put your mind to it. The more I think about it, the more convinced I am Miss Richmond is the ideal match for you.' He raised an eyebrow and she laughed. 'I swear there is not another woman in the country who would have refused you as she did. Also, I doubt there is another young lady who is brave enough to speak plainly. Yes — Miss Richmond will do very well, despite the irregular nature of your betrothal.'

'I thank you for your approval, sister. Before I vanish to my study, do not forget that we shall all be going to the Lawsons' musicale tonight. You must take your own carriage; I am collecting Lydia in mine.'

He strolled away, chuckling to himself. He believed the events of the past two days had been turned from a disaster to a triumph. Margaret was correct in her assessment of the situation. Lydia was the perfect choice for him — only now did he understand why he had never made a push to find a wife. He had been harbouring a secret love these past few years for this volatile young lady. He had kept this knowledge hidden even from himself until she was fully grown. She might not know it yet, but he was almost certain she returned his feelings. Why else would she behave in such a contrary manner when in his company? If she truly despised him, surely she would be indifferent and not react as she had been?

The next few weeks were going to be lively and he felt rejuvenated, like a young buck and not a jaded man with nothing to look forward to.

9

'Are you sure you are comfortable with me travelling alone in a closed carriage with the duke, Mama?'

'If I had any qualms, my love, I can assure you I would not have allowed you to go with him. Anyway, Lord Richmond and I will be right behind you and the journey to the Lawsons' is barely half an hour.'

Lydia was waiting in the drawing-room with her mother and her uncle. This was the first opportunity she had had to view her potential step-papa properly. He was somewhat taller than her father had been, of slimmer build, but had the same green eyes — replicas of her own. His hair was nut-brown and strangely held not a single strand of silver. He was still a handsome man, and so obviously besotted with Mama.

'Lydia, I believe I heard a carriage

arriving. If you have no objection, I shall escort you. I wish the duke to know you are not unprotected.'

'Thank you, my lord. I shall be grateful to have your company.' She turned to her mother, who was drifting around the drawing-room, the vision of loveliness in a blue silk evening gown and daring décolletage. Tonight there were no turbans or egret feathers on display: mama's hair was as stylishly arranged as her own. What a transformation! Tonight they did indeed look more like sisters than a daughter and parent.

'I'm hoping that by going out immediately it will save him from coming inside.' She rested her hand lightly on her uncle's arm and he guided her expertly through the vestibule and out into the chill of the late October evening. One of their own footmen had already lowered the steps and she was handed in without having spoken to her escort for the evening.

The steps were folded up, the door

closed, and she settled onto the squabs, expecting at any moment for the man sitting in the far corner to greet her. When he continued to remain silent she was puzzled, then became annoyed. 'Sinclair, is my arrival of so little interest to you that you intend to ignore me?'

His rich, deep chuckle filled the darkness. 'Good evening, my dear, I fear I dozed off. After all, as you so kindly pointed out to me, I'm no longer in my prime.'

She snorted inelegantly. 'Two can play games, sir, and you have only yourself to blame if you do not like the rules.'

The carriage rocked alarmingly as he sat up and shifted so his knees were touching hers. 'Is that a challenge, Lydia?' His words were soft but she detected an edge of steel behind them. For a moment she thought that maybe she had better forget her plan, as he would be a dangerous man to thwart. Then he laughed again and sat back.

'Be careful, sweetheart. I think you have met your match in me. I shall meet like for like.'

The wretched man yawned loudly, sighed, stretched out his legs and pretended to fall asleep again. She was tempted to kick his shins but knew the exercise would prove more damaging to herself than him; her evening slippers would make no impression, as he was wearing the modern fashion of trousers and slippers, not knee breeches and stockings. She supposed she should not have been surprised — after all, did he not have his hair cut short?

If he was to feign sleep then so would she. She closed her eyes and the gentle rocking of the carriage did indeed send her into the land of nod. She was jolted awake when he roared in her ear as if she were stone deaf.

'Miss Richmond, we have arrived. I suggest you get yourself together.'

Thoroughly discomfited, she answered with some asperity, 'Your Grace, it is not I that am in my dotage. There is no need to shout.' The carriage door was flung open and the bright light of the flambeaux illuminated the interior. She was not surprised to find him glaring at her, not at all the expression of a devoted future husband. At that moment the decision was made. Her plan would go ahead, and what better time to start play-acting than now, when there were a dozen footmen and several other couples making their way to the handsome modern house.

'I shall wait until you have descended, Your Grace; and then, if you would be so kind, perhaps you would assist me?' He could hardly refuse or make a pithy retort, as her crystal-clear diction carried her words to all those within earshot.

He stepped out and turned. 'Allow me to help you down, Miss Richmond.' He held out his arm, expecting her to rest her hand lightly upon it and move daintily from the step to the path. However, she pretended to stumble and fell headlong, obliging him to catch her. Anyone observing this might well have thought them to be embracing.

'I beg your pardon. How very clumsy of me, I do declare.'

His muttered response made her ears burn and she made sure she trod heavily on his instep as he swung her none too gently to the ground. Tonight was going to be an exhilarating evening, which made a change, as from bitter experience she knew the Lawsons' musicales were usually excruciatingly boring. The entertainment consisted of indifferent singing and appalling instrumentals. To her certain knowledge, there had never been anyone employed of a professional nature who would have made sitting squashed together on hard wooden chairs in a draughty ballroom bearable.

She had not released her hold on his arm; she was going to remain at his side come what may. She didn't simper or smile in a sickly fashion, for that would be alerting him too soon. It had been his idea to give the impression this was a love match, so he had nobody to blame but himself for what was about to transpire.

'Lady Alice is to introduce me to Captain Duvall tonight, Your Grace. He is the officer she met at the assembly last week.'

'Are you suggesting that I must be introduced as well?' From his tone it was obvious he disliked the prospect.

'No, sir, I am not. But I must be civil; after all, she is my closest friend. There is absolutely no necessity for you to speak to him at all.'

He stared suspiciously at her and she met his gaze. What he saw must have convinced him she was not deliberately excluding him for some reason. 'I wish you to spend time with my family. My sister and brothers are eager to further their acquaintance with my betrothed.' He ran his fingers over her left hand and frowned. 'You are not wearing your ring.' Then he half-smiled and nodded. 'Of course, it would not fit beneath your gloves.'

She had not deliberately ignored his

instruction. She had done no more than glance inside and seen an ornate and ugly diamond cluster, not at all to her taste, so she had tossed the box as casually as he had earlier onto her dressing table and promptly forgotten all about it. As he had answered his own question she had no need to lie, which was a relief as she had no wish to add prevarication to the list of misdemeanours she was intending to commit tonight.

He untied the ribbons on her evening cloak and then handed it to a waiting maid. This was the first opportunity she had had to see him in his evening rig. He looked magnificent. Black suited him, and the whiteness of his intricately tied cravat rested on a blue silk waistcoat. The colour exactly matched his eyes, as did the sapphire stick-pin that held his necktie secure.

He smiled down at her. 'Do I pass muster, my dear?'

'Absolutely. You look every inch the Duke of Stenning.' She stepped away so he could see her properly. 'And do I? I took particular pains in my appearance tonight, as this was to be our first as an engaged couple.'

'You look enchanting as always, my dear.' He drew her closer and placed her hand on his arm. 'Although, if I am strictly truthful, I'm not sure that is the adjective I would use for your appearance in the boathouse.'

She giggled. 'I don't believe anyone would have mistaken you for an aristocrat on that occasion, so hopefully we are even on that score.'

Satisfied with her comment, he led her forward through the throng, nodding and smiling as guests greeted them. Whilst he was occupied she began her charade. She glanced repeatedly at him, widening her eyes and letting a happy smile play around her lips. When anyone spoke directly to her she answered sensibly but leaned a little closer to him, making sure no one could be in any doubt she was with the love of her life.

They had progressed halfway across the entrance hall when she saw Alice beckoning to her from an alcove. 'Your Grace, Lady Alice wishes to speak to me urgently. Please excuse me; I shall join you before the entertainment starts.' Not giving him time to protest, she removed her hand from his arm and slipped away.

'Lydia, Captain Duvall is waiting to meet you. We thought it best if this did not take place in public.'

'His Grace made no objection when I told him I was to meet your captain tonight. Do your parents know you are introducing him to me?'

Alice shook her head. 'They did not come this evening. Papa has the gout and Mama would not come without him. Miss Bailey has accompanied me instead.'

'And where is your companion? I take it she is not with your captain?'

'I have sent her to find us suitable seats. Come along; we do not have much time before we have to take our places in the audience.'

Lydia was at a loss to know why she had to meet Captain Duvall in this clandestine way. There was something havey-cavey about all this. She followed her friend down a passageway and then into a small anteroom. An officer in full regimentals was pacing the floor. She had time to see he was above average height, had a good physique and beautiful corn-coloured hair.

'My love, I was beginning to despair of you.' The smile he gave Alice convinced Lydia that the young man was genuinely attached to her friend. 'Miss Richmond, I'm delighted to make your acquaintance. Captain Adam Duvall at your service.' He bowed deeply and she curtsied in reply. He really was a delightful gentleman.

'Captain Duvall, I have heard so much about you from Lady Alice. Will you be stationed at Weeley Barracks for the remainder of the war?'

'Sadly, I fear not. We are training up a

new battalion. The recruits will ship out to Spain in the spring and I shall go with them.' Alice looked stricken at his news. Immediately he took her hands and smiled lovingly. 'We have almost six months together — a lot can change in that time.'

The sound of a bell being rung indicated the start of the concert. 'We must hurry, Alice. I have no wish to keep the duke waiting.' Leaving the two of them, she scurried back to the vestibule, praying there would still be several couples as tardy as she. There was only one person waiting, and he didn't seem overjoyed to see her.

She skidded to a halt beside him and tendered her apologies. 'I do beg your pardon, Your Grace. I had no idea I had been so long.' She risked a quick glance in his direction and saw that his eyes were laughing, even though his expression was stern.

'As far as I'm concerned, sweetheart, I would happily wait here until the wretched thing was quite over. However, as you have arrived, I suppose we must go in and have our sensibilities and ears tortured for the next two hours.'

'It won't be as long as that, sir, Mama told me Lady Lawson has been let down by several of her performers. With luck we shall escape in no more than an hour.'

'Praise be! If her ladyship asks for volunteers from the audience I shall give them my best basilisk stare. Hopefully that will be enough to stem their enthusiasm. Tell me again, my dear, why we agreed to come here?'

'Hush, Sinclair. Someone will hear you. Look, Mama has saved us two seats on the back row. We will be able to take our places without disturbing anyone else.'

After an hour of caterwauling and indifferent piano playing, the concert came to an end. The audience clapped politely and rose as one body to make a dash for the exits. Lydia watched them rush past. In their eagerness to escape, some of the little gilt chairs tumbled to the ground.

Lord Richmond, who had been sitting adjacent to the duke, shook his head in bafflement. 'Why do people come when they know the entertainment will be dire?'

'Lady Lawson has the best chef in the neighbourhood; her buffet suppers are legendary. No one refuses an invitation to come here, however bad the singing.' Her mother rose gracefully and nodded at the duke. 'I fear we will be too late to find an empty table. Shall we take a turn around the ballroom until there is room?'

'There will be a table for us. Lady Margaret will already be seated.' The duke offered his arm and Lydia took it. A footman hesitated beside them with a tray of champagne and Lydia took a glass — she had a feeling she might need something to distract her.

'Does that mean, Your Grace, that once I am your duchess I shall never have to wait for anything?' She fluttered her eyelashes and he laughed.

He bent his head and whispered in her ear, 'You are a saucy minx, my dear. I can see that you have been spoilt by your parents. I shall enjoy teaching you how to behave.'

'And I, sir, shall enjoy watching you fail.'

His shout of laughter caused several people to turn in their direction and she took the opportunity to gaze adoringly at him as if she worshipped the very ground he stood on. Unfortunately they were at that very moment walking past an over-mantel mirror. His eyes narrowed and her hand was trapped between his elbow and his side.

'Lady Richmond, Lord Richmond, pray excuse us for a moment. There is something I want to say to your daughter before we go into supper. Would you kindly inform my party that we shall join them in a few moments?'

Lydia watched in horror as her mother vanished into the dining room, leaving her to her fate. He marched her through the nearest open door and closed it firmly behind him.

'What in God's name are you playing at? Have you been doing this all night?'

'You said we were to appear a love match — I was just following your instructions.'

'People will either think I am marrying a simpleton or a young lady with no decorum. The play-acting was to start after we were married, as well you know.'

She shrugged and took a sip from her glass as if unmoved by his question. She had trodden on the tail of a very large panther. She straightened her shoulders. She would not apologise. If she started now, she would be forever begging his pardon, and that would make her life intolerable. 'I believe, sir, that you once told me a duke is above reproach. I must assume that by marrying you I am now included in this strange situation. Therefore my decorum, or lack of it, can be of no importance to either of us.'

The matter hung in the balance. His look would have shrivelled a lesser person, but she would not be cowed. She refused to look away and matched him stare for stare. The silence stretched. If he did not speak soon she would collapse in an ignominious heap, as her legs were shaking as much as her hands. Then her glass shattered, the noise shockingly loud. She could not bite back her yelp of pain as splinters embedded themselves in her palms.

'Let me see. No, sweetheart, give me your hands — show me what you have done.' Gently he uncurled her fingers and his shocked exclamation made her glance down. Her gloves were scarlet, the shards of glass sticking through the soft kid leather. She clapped her gloves to her face. The pain made her head swim. She never could abide the sight of blood. A swirling blackness filled her head and she toppled forward.

★ ★ ★

Aubrey caught her as she fell and carried her across to a convenient sofa. He swore under his breath as he carefully picked out the glass from the gore-soaked gloves in order to examine the extent of the injury. By so doing he transferred the goodly part of her blood to himself. After removing the gloves he realised the injuries were not as bad as he'd feared. The bleeding was already less now that he had draped her hands over the back of the sofa. Hastily unwinding his neck cloth, he tore it in half and quickly bound each hand.

Two of the cuts might need sutures but she was in no danger; the injuries looked far worse than they actually were. The duke smiled ruefully as he sat back on his heels. They both looked as if they had been on the battlefront. Lydia's eyes were flickering; she was about to come round.

He needed something to clean them both up. He quickly tore off a large strip from her chemise. This would be ideal for the purpose — but first he needed water to dampen it. There was an impressive arrangement of hothouse flowers on a side table. Without a thought to the consequences, he upended it and soaked the cloth in the puddle. Ignoring the scattered flowers and leaves, he began to wipe the worst of the blood from Lydia's arms and face. There was nothing he could do about the unpleasant stains on her lovely gown, but at least he could clean her up so she wouldn't swoon again from shock. Neither could he remove the gore from his waistcoat and shirt front.

Suddenly the door flew open and Lord and Lady Richmond burst in. The lady screamed and the lord surged forward. 'What have you done, you villain — have you murdered my niece?'

10

Lydia came round to pandemonium. Her mother was sobbing loudly and her uncle stood beside her, glaring down at the prostrate figure of her betrothed. She pushed herself up on to her elbows. 'What on earth is going on? What are you doing on the floor, Sinclair?'

Lord Richmond leapt into the air as if stabbed by a pin, and her mother froze mid-sob. The duke scrambled to his feet, rubbing his jaw. Lydia stared from one to the other in bewilderment. Her relatives looked at her as if she were a ghost. The duke grinned lopsidedly and raised an eyebrow.

'My darling daughter, we thought you were dead and that . . . ' Her mother was unable to finish her sentence.

'My injuries were caused by a broken glass. Sinclair was taking care of me;

that is how he comes to be in such disarray.'

Her uncle shook his head and looked up in bafflement. 'He was . . . you were — '

'I accept your apology for knocking me down, Lord Richmond. I would've done the same thing if I had thought a relative of mine injured.'

No apology had been tendered and her uncle seemed in no mood to offer one. The duke was attempting to defuse the situation. 'Mama, my lord, this has been a huge misunderstanding,' Lydia said. 'As you can see I have cut my hands, ruined my gown and, in ministering to me, His Grace has also spoiled his appearance. Obviously we must leave — but it might be prudent for you to return to the entertainment before we attract any more attention.'

The duke had turned away and she was almost sure from his rigid stance that he was trying not to laugh.

'I shall do as you suggest, my love.' Her mother looked crossly at the duke.

She raised her voice as if by turning away he had become hard of hearing. 'I shall leave you to escort my daughter home and arrange for the physician to call, Your Grace. I shall make your apologies to our hostess.'

He finally managed to control his amusement and swung round. 'Could I kindly ask you to inform my sister what has transpired here, Lady Richmond? Also, if you could send in a footman I should be most obliged.'

'This is most irregular, Your Grace. I should not have given my consent to your betrothal if I'd known what was going to happen. Come along, Richmond. We have errands to run and I do not wish to miss my supper.'

The door closed loudly behind them. 'Botheration! Mama is most upset with us. It will take a deal of smoothing over tomorrow to put things right.' Lydia scowled at him. 'This is your fault, you know, Sinclair. If we are to carry on in this fashion, one or the other of us will be in the grave by the end of the year.'

She had been going to hold up her hands and count on her fingers the number of occasions she had been injured since she had become involved with him, but thought better of it when she saw the blood seeping through his hastily constructed bandages. She flopped back, closing her eyes and waiting for the dizziness to pass.

'Silly goose — I would never have thought a girl as brave as you would have a fit of the vapours at the sight of blood.' He gently stroked the hair from her sticky cheeks.

'What is that peculiar smell?'

He chuckled. 'That will be the water from the flower arrangement — I used it to clean the worst of the gore from your face and arms.'

The situation was beyond ridiculous. 'I see you are not denying my suggestion, Your Grace. First you ruined my gown, then drove me from your house in the middle of the night, then attempted to drown me, and tonight you stabbed me with a glass.

Hardly a promising start.' Her voice wobbled and a snort of laughter escaped, quite ruining her reprimand.

When the butler and a maidservant came in, they found the couple quite helpless with laughter. The duke recovered his equanimity first. 'Kindly have my carriage brought round forthwith and fetch Miss Richmond's cloak at once. I require you to inform me when the vestibule is empty — we have no wish to upset any of the Lady Lawson's guests by our dishevelled appearance.'

'At once, Your Grace. Might I suggest that I send a footman to alert the doctor?'

'Excellent suggestion. He must attend at Ravenscroft immediately.' He offered his hand to Lydia. 'Do you feel well enough to walk, or shall I carry you?'

'Heaven forfend! I am quite capable of walking, thank you, Your Grace.' To prove the point she stood up, making sure she put no pressure on her injured hands. She was sure she would be at no risk of collapse as long as she kept her injuries out of sight. 'There you are. I am ready to go as soon as my cloak is on.'

He carefully arranged the garment around her shoulders and tied the ribbon at the neck. 'You cannot hold onto me, sweetheart, so I must put my arm around your waist to support you. You still look very shaky.'

She was grateful for his strength, for her limbs appeared to have a will of their own. The butler escorted them across the deserted hallway and two footmen were waiting by the carriage in case their assistance was needed. When the duke tightened his hold and placed his other arm beneath her knees, she did not protest. He carefully lifted her inside and jumped in behind her. Instead of sitting as he had before on the far side of the carriage, he sat beside her. 'Lean on me. I will keep you safe on the journey. You must not use your hands to steady you when we hit a rut or pothole in the lane.'

It was surprisingly comfortable resting her head on his shoulder and having his arm around her waist. Her hands throbbed unpleasantly and she was developing a sick headache. She closed her eyes, trying not to think about what was to come. Having her wounds sewn together, however necessary, was not an experience she was looking forward to.

★ ★ ★

Aubrey felt her relax and knew she had fallen asleep. He eased himself across the squabs, taking her with him so that her head was in his lap. The carriage rocked and bumped and at each jolt he tightened his grip, making sure she didn't slip.

She was right to blame him for this misadventure. If he had not been so angry at her play-acting, the accident would not have happened — to have broken the glass as she did must have taken considerable strength. In fact, she was correct: since he had trodden on her dress she had suffered a series of accidents which would not have occurred if he had not been involved.

The coach slowed and swung through the gates of Ravenscroft; they would be arriving very soon, so had he better rouse her? No, he would carry her inside and take her up to her apartment. The housekeeper and her maid could do the rest.

When they were stationary he was ready. Slowly he eased her on to his lap, made sure he had a secure grip, and ducked through the door, almost falling when he trod on a sharp stone. Dammit to hell! These ridiculous evening slippers were not the footwear for an active man.

He was ushered through the house and along the corridor by the housekeeper. 'If you would be so kind as to bring Miss Richmond into her chamber, I shall take care of her then. Will the doctor be attending?'

'Yes, he should be here very soon.

Miss Richmond cut her hands on a broken glass and has been somewhat overwhelmed by the experience.'

'Oh dear me! Even as a little girl she would faint clean away if she cut herself.'

Two girls had already turned down the bed so he gently placed her there. 'I shall wait next door for the doctor.' As he was leaving the room Lydia called him back.

'Your Grace, thank you for helping me this evening. I am feeling much better now I am at home; when I am cleaned up and respectable I shall come through. Doctor Jacobs can attend to me there.'

He was tempted to return to her side but he restrained himself. He had no wish to frighten her with his unwanted attentions; time enough once they were man and wife. 'Do not get up if you are feeling at all unwell, my dear.' He smiled and for once she responded. Something strange happened to his chest — it was as if a giant hand had squeezed it, pushing all his breath away. He gripped the door frame to steady himself. 'As you are decidedly squeamish, it might be safer if you are already prone.'

'Go away, you wretch. A more considerate gentleman would not have drawn attention to my unfortunate tendency to faint at the sight of blood.'

He left her to be taken care of by her maids and wandered into her private sitting-room. He had already invaded her privacy, but on his previous visit had not had time to examine the chamber thoroughly. One could tell a great deal about a person from their personal possessions.

The room was well appointed: a daybed, two padded armchairs and a small sofa were set in a square in front of the handsome fireplace. They were all covered in some sort of shiny material in an attractive shade of green, and the drapes echoed this colour. There was a small desk, the chair neatly arranged in front; and, if he was not mistaken, there was a deep, comfortable window seat behind the curtains. There were four pretty watercolours on one wall, but the other was entirely filled with shelves upon which were countless books.

He was about to examine the spines when he heard hurrying footsteps outside. The physician must be here. He strode to the door and flung it open. 'Good man — come in — Miss Richmond will be through as soon as she is changed.'

The portly gentleman stopped so abruptly he almost tipped on to his nose. 'Your Grace, I did not . . . I mean, I had not expected — '

'Miss Richmond and I are betrothed. We are to be married next month.'

The doctor flushed, bowed deeply, and mumbled some sort of apology. 'I was told that Miss Richmond needed sutures. I am tardy because I boiled my instruments before leaving. I have found that my patients fare better when I adopt this procedure.' The bed

chamber door opened and Lydia
appeared.

* * *

'I should dearly like a bath, Jenny, but
with my hands bandaged as they are I
don't think this would be a practical
option. However, I do need to remove
both the blood and the evil-smelling
water from my person.'

Her maid efficiently took off Lydia's
ruined evening gown and then sponged
her down in warm water. 'There, miss.
You are sweet-smelling and clean again.
Will you put on a morning gown, or
something else?'

'I might as well put on my nightgown
and bedrobe; the doctor is well used to
seeing ladies in a state of undress, and
as the duke and I are to be married
shortly I hardly think it matters to him
either.'

She would not be dissuaded from
this decision. With such sore hands it
would be uncomfortable and tiresome

to don the required underpinnings necessary for day clothes. Therefore it made perfect sense to slip on a soft lawn nightgown and preserve her decency by wearing a wrapper over the top. Indeed, when she viewed herself in the glass, she decided there was less of her visible than there had been in her evening gown.

'I believe the doctor is here, Miss Richmond,' a chambermaid called out from the dressing room. 'Will I fetch him in to you?'

★ ★ ★

'No, thank you. I am going into my parlour for treatment.' Lydia was obliged to wait for Jenny to open the door before she could enter. Doctor Jacobs and the duke turned towards her. The expression on Sinclair's face was an image she would never forget. If she had danced in totally undressed he could not have looked more shocked.

'Here I am, gentlemen, as ready as I

ever will be to have my hands examined and stitched.'

The physician was unbothered by her appearance and bowed. 'Would you like to sit on this upright chair, Miss Richmond? I can use this side table for my instruments.'

Sinclair recovered his voice. 'You should not have come out here as you are — '

'That is fustian, Your Grace. I cannot imagine anyone objecting to my being in my nightwear in my own apartment.' She smiled sweetly. 'However, the fact that you are also in here might well be viewed with extreme disfavour.'

'I have no intention of leaving until I know your hands are not severely damaged.'

The doctor had taken her left hand and was carefully unwrapping the makeshift bandage. Lydia kept her gaze averted. 'A clean cut, Miss Richmond, and I do not think it requires stitching. It has already stopped bleeding; all it requires is a dressing.'

Whilst he busied himself doing this she resumed her conversation with the duke. 'And, Your Grace, if my hands had been disfigured, would you have withdrawn your offer?'

'Absolutely — one cannot have a wife who is not perfect in every aspect.'

His reply shocked her; then she saw his mouth twitch and knew he was teasing her. 'I am delighted to hear that apart from my injured hands you consider me 'perfect in every aspect'.'

'Indeed I do, my dear, which is fortuitous as the entire neighbourhood is aware how much you dote on me.'

The doctor interrupted their badinage. 'There you are, Miss Richmond. All done. Now I shall attend to your right hand.' His sharp intake of breath made her look and she wished she hadn't. This cut was far deeper and still oozing. Her head began to swim.

'Look at me, sweetheart. Let Doctor Jacobs do his job.' Sinclair crouched beside her and gently turned her face away.

'I know it is silly to be so affected, but ever since I fell and put my teeth through my lower lip I have been unable to stay conscious when faced with blood.'

'So we shall talk of something else until this is done. What would you like as a wedding gift? I thought perhaps a racing phaeton would be something you would like.'

'Have you run mad? I would not climb onto one of those contraptions even with you holding the ribbons.'

A sharp pain in her palm made her catch her breath. Immediately he reached out to stroke her face. His unexpected gesture distracted her and she jerked her head away. 'I know what I should like for a wedding gift, sir. A puppy of my own. Mama cannot abide indoor pets and I have always wanted a dog — preferably a large and shaggy one.'

He chuckled. 'Is that all? No diamonds? No new gowns? I am staggered at your economy, my dear.

However, I already have a dog — Juno. You have met him. I'm afraid he might not take kindly to an interloper.'

She swallowed the bile in her throat as the doctor continued to prod and probe, sending waves of pain shooting up her arm. The chair back was too low for her to rest her head and she did so want to close her eyes until the procedure was over.

'Lean on me, sweetheart. The doctor will soon be done.' He knelt beside her and put his arm around her shoulders. His solid strength supported her and she couldn't resist his suggestion. She sagged sideways into his embrace and allowed the swirling darkness to take over.

* * *

She woke the next day in her own bed to find her mother sitting beside her. 'How are you feeling, my love? You have given us all a nasty shock, for you have been unconscious for hours.'

'How silly of me! The duke must think me a feeble girl indeed.'

'Indeed he does not. He was pacing up and down the drawing-room most of the night. He would not let poor Doctor Jacobs leave until your swoon turned into a deep slumber.'

'Is he still here?'

'No, he departed with the doctor at dawn.'

Lydia attempted to sit up but her sore hands prevented her. 'Have you been sitting here all night? You must be so tired, Mama. Please go to bed, I am perfectly well now.'

'Let me help you, my dear. Then after I feed you your breakfast, I shall retire.'

Lydia had no wish to be fed like a baby. She would rather go hungry. 'No, there is no need. I have no appetite this morning, but when I do wish to eat Jenny can help me.'

Her mother pushed herself wearily from the chair and bent forward to kiss Lydia on the forehead. 'In which case, I shall take your advice and go to my chamber. By the way, I can't tell you how pleased I am that you are now happy with your betrothal. Everyone was saying your relationship with the duke has to be a love match.'

11

Lydia was in no position to deny this statement — after all, had she not set out to convince the guests she was besotted with the duke? 'We are both much happier about the situation than we were last week. However, calling it a love match is rather premature.'

Her mother smiled archly. 'It is of no matter, my dear. You have the rest of your lives to fall in love. Now, I shall do as you suggest. I have left word downstairs that you are not receiving. I shall see you later on.'

As soon as her mother drifted out, Jenny appeared. 'Miss Richmond, Lady Alice is downstairs and is most insistent that she see you. Shall I send her away?'

'No, I would like to see her.' Her stomach gurgled loudly. 'Perhaps Cook has some cake or scones I could eat more easily than a full meal. Please send word to the kitchen for me.'

Within a short space of time both Alice and the cake arrived. After commiserating with Lydia, Alice settled herself on the end of the bed. 'I have such extraordinary news for you. The duke came to see Papa yesterday and now my anniversary ball is to be held at Stenning Hall. We are to share the occasion — it is now to celebrate your wedding as well.'

'That's an excellent idea. I don't know why I didn't suggest it to him myself. The ballroom at Stenning is twice the size of yours so we can have twice as many guests.'

'Papa has refused to countenance any officers being invited. Both he and my mother have now decided that as you are about to become a bride they must find me a suitable husband too.'

'I am sure that Mama can invite whomsoever she pleases — you have a list of names you would like me to include on our guest list?' Lydia smiled as her friend immediately removed a piece of folded paper and handed it over.

'I shall send this down to her immediately. If she queries my wish to have seven cavalry officers attend, I shall tell her I wish all the single ladies be able to have an unattached gentleman to dance with. After all, we will be celebrating my nuptials as well as your name day and neither of us would wish to see a row of wallflowers.'

Alice nodded vigourously. 'Indeed, Lydia, I agree with you on every count. It would be a sad sight indeed when we will both be so happy.'

They spent a pleasant hour together before Alice departed, promising to call again in a day or two. The list of names had been taken downstairs by Jenny and so far there had been no adverse comments. Doctor Jacobs called and checked both hands.

'I shall remove the dressing from your left hand, Miss Richmond. The cut is healing well and will benefit from being open to fresh air. I shall return in three days to remove the sutures from the other hand. As you are left-handed, I am sure you will find things much easier now.'

'How long will it be before I can ride? Will my hands remain tender for a long time?'

'No, Miss Richmond. As you ride in gloves there should be no problem at all. As soon as the stitches are removed it will be for you to decide.'

He departed, leaving her to return to the book she had abandoned a few days before. The weather had turned from crisp autumnal dryness to damp and dismal. She doubted she would be able to ride even when her hands were recovered.

★   ★   ★

The following day Lydia rose at her usual time and dressed in her favourite promenade gown. This was in a dark green stripe and had a matching spencer. Jenny carefully tied the ribbons to the delightful bonnet that accompanied the ensemble, and she was ready for her walk. 'I am not quite sure about this ensemble, Jenny. I must own that I feel a trifle overdressed.'

'Oh no, miss. You look a picture. You never know who you might meet on your return.'

Lydia could not deny she had taken particular attention with her appearance this morning just in case Sinclair came to visit. It would not do for him to think she was dowdy.

The rain had stopped and the sun was out, a perfect day for a brisk stroll around the grounds. She enjoyed her perambulation and was quite exhilarated by her excursion. On her return she discovered a smart blue-wheeled gig, drawn by a handsome black gelding, waiting outside the front door. This was not a vehicle she recognised. She was mounting the steps when the door swung open and Sinclair stepped out.

'Excellent; I was coming out to find

you. I have come to take you for a drive.' He smiled and gestured towards the carriage. 'Do you like it, sweetheart?'

She walked over and ran her gloved hand over the smooth, shiny side. 'I love it, Your Grace. I don't believe I've ever seen you drive a gig.'

'I purchased it for you. Today I shall demonstrate how to drive it, and as soon as your hands are mended you shall take the ribbons. You are an excellent horsewoman so I am quite certain driving this vehicle will present no difficulties.'

Although this carriage was not as precarious as a high perch-phaeton, the wheels were still considerably larger than they were on a normal travelling coach. This was also open to the elements, and so not something to be used during the winter.

'There is room for only two of us, Your Grace, and if it rains we shall get wet.'

'Very observant, my dear. I knew I

was marrying a young lady of high intelligence. Hurry up; I do not wish to keep the horse standing any longer.'

She moved to the side where the step was but before she could place a foot on it, he had grasped her from behind and hoisted her into the air as if she weighed no more than a bag of feathers. The gig was remarkably stable and only rocked a little.

'Thank you for your assistance, Your Grace, but next time you are going to sling me into a carriage could you give me due warning?'

His laughter startled both the horse and the groom standing at his head. The duke ignored the rumpus and jumped aboard, picking up the reins and whip. 'Are you settled, Miss Richmond?' She nodded and he flicked the whip above the horse's ears. Immediately the carriage moved forward smoothly.

Once they were away from eavesdroppers, she turned to him. 'Are we going anywhere in particular, Your

Grace? Or are we just going for a drive in the country?' He ignored her comment and she stiffened with annoyance. 'I asked you a question, Your Grace — '

Without glancing in her direction he answered. 'And I am not going to respond until you address me as we agreed.'

'If you insist, Sinclair. I shall ask you again. Are we going — '

Again he rudely interrupted her. 'I think it is fair to say that the answer to both your questions is yes. As to where we are driving you will have to wait and see.'

She scowled at his profile and was tempted to poke him sharply in the ribs but thought better of it. Not that she was worried by how he might react, but because she had no wish to distract him and cause an accident. She settled onto the comfortable seat and looked around her. They were already bowling along a lane she seldom used — she was almost certain it led to one of the duke's farms.

The hedge was too high to allow her to see the countryside and too narrow to be able to pass an oncoming vehicle. 'What happens if we meet another carriage?'

'I shall require them to get out of my way, of course.'

Shocked by his answer, she spoke without thinking. 'Just because you are the landowner does not mean you can . . . can . . . ' she stuttered to a halt. He was laughing at her again. 'You are a most objectionable gentleman, and I hope you fall off into the nearest dung heap.'

He grinned, quite unrepentant. 'And I hope that the next time I take you for a drive you are not wearing such an ugly bonnet.'

'My bonnet is the first stare of fashion. The milliner copied it from a fashion plate sent down from London.' She intended to elaborate on the excellence of her headwear but he stopped her.

'That's as may be, my dear, but the

brim is so deep it resembles a coal scuttle and I cannot see your face inside it. Whatever possessed you to put it on just for walking in the park?'

She giggled. She could hardly deny his accusation. 'I shall take it off at once. I believe that it's quite the silliest bonnet I've ever purchased.' Without allowing him to protest she undid the bow at her neck, and in a moment of abandon tossed it over the hedge.

'Good grief, Lydia. I did not want you to throw it away. What a pea goose you are.' He pulled on the reins and guided the gig to a halt by a five-barred gate. 'I suppose I must ruin my boots by scrambling into the field to recover your coal scuttle.'

She grabbed his arm, shocked at how hard it was beneath her fingers. 'There's no need for you to put yourself out on my account, Sinclair. Leave it where it is; I shall never wear it again.'

'Absolutely not. If you don't wish to wear it, then you can give it to someone who will appreciate its value.' He sounded distinctly unimpressed by her actions and, after pulling on the brake, he handed her the ribbons and jumped down into the lane.

Not bothering to open the gate, he placed one hand on the top bar and vaulted over it. For a member of the aristocracy he was remarkably fit — she must ask him how this came to be. His hat was visible on the other side of the hedge and she could hear him talking to somebody or something. Were there cows in the field, or maybe horses? She decided to stand up so she could see. She was not quite tall enough, but if she stood on the seat she would definitely be above the hedge.

She spoke to the horse waiting patiently, obviously unbothered by being stopped in the lane. Carefully gripping the wooden struts along the back seat with her good hand, she stepped up. The carriage wobbled but not enough to unbalance her. Sinclair had vanished from view. The animals he had been conversing with were a small herd of heifers; for some reason they were gathered against the hedge so their heads were not visible.

'Sinclair, what is happening over there?' Lydia's voice carried beautifully, startling the beasts, and with a deal of mooing and grunting they scattered in all directions. There was still no sign of her companion; she did hope he had not been trampled. She stood on tiptoe, hoping to get a glimpse of him. Just as she was precariously positioned, the horse moved forward. The result was inevitable.

With a screech of despair, she toppled backwards from the vehicle into the equally dense hedge that ran on the opposite side of the narrow lane.

★   ★   ★

Aubrey had been about to pick up the missing item when she had called out. The nearest heifer barged into him and he ended up on his knees in a cowpat. Incensed at the indignity, he dropped her bonnet. When she cried out he guessed at once what had happened. He was up and over the gate in seconds. Where the hell was she? The horse flicked his ears and nudged him in the shoulder. Only then did he hear muffled shouts for help coming from the other side of the carriage.

'Keep still, sweetheart. You will make matters worse if you wriggle like that.' Thank God she wasn't seriously injured. She could not be making so much noise if she was. 'I shall have you out of there in no time.'

He thought she said something about killing him, but he must have misheard. He always carried a thin knife in its scabbard tucked into the top of his boot — a useful trick he had adopted on the Peninsula and still continued to this day. The hedge was now still and he parted the branches to see his beloved securely trapped in the very centre of the hedge. She must have landed bottom first and her weight had taken her down so she was firmly wedged, but fortunately the right way up.

'You are an imbecile. You could have killed me by your stupidity.' She glared at him and he was fairly sure if her hands had been free she would have punched him squarely on the nose. 'Get me out of here at once.'

'I am about to do so, my dear.' He was doing his best not to smile, as she looked so silly with her hair tumbling over her shoulders and liberally covered with twigs and leaves. 'I am relieved you're not hurt, but mystified as to how you fell into the hedge rather than the lane.'

Her lips thinned and she quivered with rage. However, she thought better of whatever she had been going to say and remained silent. Ten minutes of hacking and swearing and she was free. He reached in and lifted her out; with her still in his arms, he pivoted and placed her gently on the seat.

In the corner of his eye he saw her left fist clench and reacted swiftly. He caught her wrist before the blow connected. 'I do not recommend you recourse to fisticuffs, Miss Richmond. As you have told me many times before, I do not behave as a gentleman.'

He maintained his hold until she relaxed, not taking his gaze from hers for a moment. Her beautiful green eyes seemed larger somehow, her lips softer and her wonderful hair an invitation. He couldn't help himself. He stepped on to the foot plate and drew her closer.

She recoiled and shoved him hard in the chest. 'What is that dreadful smell?'

He had barely maintained his balance and was in danger of losing his temper. He drew breath to castigate her and gagged. 'Tarnation! I had forgotten I fell into manure.'

She peered over the side of the gig and a gurgle of laughter escaped. 'Good heavens! Your unmentionables are . . . quite unmentionable!'

His anger evaporated — it was hard to remain cross with her for long. 'You might well laugh, Miss Richmond,' he said sternly, 'but remember I have to sit next to you for the remainder of the journey.' So saying, he squeezed past the rear of the vehicle and clambered aboard.

'My bonnet — all this excitement and the wretched thing is still missing.' She shuffled across the seat until she was pressed as far away as she could be from him. 'Sinclair, if you think I am continuing on this drive with you stinking like a midden, and myself in little better case, then you are sadly mistaken. Kindly turn the vehicle around at the earliest opportunity and take me home.'

'Very well, I shall do as you ask. However, I shall return this afternoon. No, do not shake your head at me young lady. You will be waiting for me at two o'clock.' She tossed her head, a gesture somewhat spoilt by the wildness of her appearance. 'If you are not waiting in the vestibule I shall come and find you.'

'And if I refuse to accompany you? What then?'

'I will sling you over my shoulder like a sack of potatoes and carry you kicking and screaming through the house if needs be.'

She tilted her head and examined his expression closely, then nodded as if satisfied. 'I have no wish to give my mother a fit of the vapours, Your Grace, so I will be waiting for you as requested.'

The remainder of the journey was completed in silence. His eyes were watering from the stench and she was in little better case. As soon as the gig was stationary she scrambled out and didn't stop until she was a goodly distance away.

'You will understand my eagerness to leave you, Your Grace. I can honestly tell you that I have never experienced such an unpleasant drive in my life.' She grinned and his spirits lifted. 'I can also tell you that it was, without doubt, the most exciting.' With a wave of her left hand she turned and ran gracefully up the steps like a wood nymph with her hair flowing about her shoulders. God knew what Lady Richmond would make of the excursion.

He could not help but notice the groom was standing at the far side of the yard. He did not blame him one jot. He clicked to the horse, flicked his whip and headed for Stenning. He was not known for his levity, nor for unpredictable behaviour — yet in this past two weeks he had been involved in more disasters and upsets than he had in his six years of soldiering. Was Lydia correct in saying that they were incompatible? That their propensity for becoming involved in joint catastrophes would mean they were heading for tragedy?

12

The house was quiet and Lydia managed to reach her apartment without being seen by anyone. Jenny greeted her with resignation. 'This is the fourth gown you have ruined in the past week, miss, I cannot imagine what has come over you lately.'

'Unfortunately we had an accident with the carriage, but neither of us was hurt. His Grace is returning to collect me at two o'clock, so we have plenty of time to wash my hair before then.' This time she was tempted to put on her oldest ensemble just in case another disaster overtook them. Jenny was scandalised at the suggestion and fetched another promenade dress similar to the first. 'I shall need the pelisse, Jenny, as there is a definite nip in the air today. Is there a less alarming bonnet I can wear?'

'The pretty chip straw with the narrow brim would be ideal, as I can trim it with ribbons to match your outfit. I believe we have an orange ribbon that would be perfect with the russet of your gown.'

When Lydia was ready she went in search of her mother. Although she had been unobserved on her return, she could not be sure Sinclair had not been seen. She found her working in the garden room with Lord Richmond.

'There you are, my love. Did you have a pleasant drive? Your uncle and I have decided we are going to continue with your papa's work.' She looked as excited as a child at a party. 'Once you are married and settled, we are going to travel the world and look for fresh specimens to plant in here.'

'Go away? You and Uncle Edward? I don't understand.'

'My dear girl, we will not be leaving until next spring at the very earliest,' he said. 'This is something I have been thinking about for some time. I intended to travel on my own, but your mother — '

Lydia looked from one to the other and decided to make things easier for them. 'I hope you will be married before you leave — one member of this family creating scandals is quite sufficient.'

Immediately her mother dropped the trowel and flung her arms around her. 'You do not mind? We would never have considered doing so if you had not been about to leave Ravenscroft yourself.'

'I am delighted that you and Uncle Edward can finally be together. I'm sure Papa would be happy too.'

Her mother stepped back and stared at Lydia. 'You have changed your gown. Are you intending to go out again today?'

'Unfortunately we had a slight mishap and could not complete our journey earlier today, so the duke is returning at two o'clock to collect me. The gig is my wedding gift — he's going to teach me to drive it.'

This information was received with exclamations of delight and her uncle and mother abandoned their gardening to accompany her to the small dining room where a light luncheon was being served. She could not remember her mother being so animated and Lydia was happy for her.

She left them planning their own wedding and could not help but contrast their relationship with hers. She swallowed a lump in her throat and thought of what she was missing. If Mama were to find out how reluctant she was to marry Sinclair, would she insist the union go ahead? Then a possible alternative occurred to her. When her uncle and mother were married, she could accompany them on their travels and, by the time they returned, society would have forgotten all about her indiscretions with Sinclair.

Should she run back and tell them first, or would it be better to break the news to the duke? How extraordinary that there should be such a simple solution to her predicament. She was not looking forward to breaking the news to her erstwhile bridegroom — and there was ample time to send out cancellations to all those who had been invited.

She had enjoyed her sparring with Sinclair, would miss his company, but she felt as if she had been set free. Knowing she did not have to marry without love would be enough to give her the courage to break off the engagement.

The duke arrived at precisely two o'clock and this time she was ready to step up into the gig without him having to descend.

'I'm glad you heeded my advice, my dear, and have worn a more sensible bonnet. You wish to take the reins? After all, this is to be your vehicle and I want you to be proficient.'

If they would not be married, there was no point in her learning to drive. 'No, thank you, Your Grace. I should much prefer to watch you. Also, my right hand is still too sore.'

'As you wish.' They were at the end of the drive before he spoke again. 'What is wrong, sweetheart?'

How could he know she was upset? She would have to tell him; it wasn't fair to keep him in ignorance of her decision. She turned on the seat so she could see his face. 'Something quite remarkable has occurred, Your Grace. My mother and Lord Richmond are to be married and are then going to travel the world collecting botanical specimens for the conservatory.'

'Are you unhappy about this? Do you not wish your uncle to become your stepfather?'

She took a deep breath. 'No, I am delighted. And so should you be, as it releases you from your obligation. I shall go with them. We will be away a year or two, and by the time we return what did or did not happen will be old gossip.'

She had expected him to congratulate her, be as pleased as she was they could avoid an unwanted union. Instead his expression changed. 'You have forgotten one thing, young lady. I am your legal guardian and you need my permission to traipse off across the world.'

★   ★   ★

His hurt had made him speak angrily. He loved her and couldn't bear the thought of losing her. He fought back his heartbreak and attempted to make his next response more reasonable. 'I am sorry, Lydia. My surprise made me respond more harshly than I intended.'

She was staring at him wide-eyed. 'I thought you would be pleased. Why would you wish to stop me?'

'I don't think you have thought this through, my dear. Have you told Lord and Lady Richmond of your plans?' She shook her head. 'I am relieved to hear you say so. Lady Richmond will immediately cancel her own plans if you are not to be married. The only reason she has agreed to such an arrangement is because she believes you are making an advantageous and happy marriage yourself.'

'I don't see why that should be so, Your Grace. Surely it is better for all of us if I go abroad? Isn't that what young ladies do when they have damaged their good name?'

What she said was perfectly true; by absenting herself from the country the reason for her travels would soon be forgotten. How could he convince her she was wrong? If she broke the engagement and vanished overseas, she might well meet somebody else and his opportunity would be gone.

'The invitations have been sent, the arrangements made, and the banns have been called for the first time. Cancelling the wedding is out of the question. I am The Duke of Stenning and I will not be made a figure of fun.' He sounded like a pompous jackass, but he could think of no other way to prevent this calamity.

'I cannot believe you wish to continue with a loveless union just to save your pride. No, I am quite decided. Even if Mama and Uncle Edward cancel their own plans, I will not marry you. I would rather be ostracised than enter into a marriage with a man I dislike and despise.'

He concentrated on negotiating the exit from Ravenscroft, keeping his face averted. He had lost her, and it was his own fault. He must never let her know she had shattered his dreams. This was a burden he would not share with anyone.

★   ★   ★

Should she demand he turn back? After all, if they were no longer to be married in two weeks, then the gig was not hers and she did not need to know how to drive it. She was about to speak when he turned back to her, his expression friendly.

'I apologise unreservedly for trying to

browbeat you into a marriage that is obviously distasteful. I will cancel the arrangements and speak to Lady Richmond on our return. If you are determined to go abroad I shall not stand in your way.'

In the face of his magnanimity she could hardly insist they cancel the drive — after all, he was her legal guardian still. 'I accept your apology and thank you for your agreement. Now, shall we talk of other matters? Where are we going?'

He blinked and rubbed his eyes as if he had a headache. 'I was taking you to one of my tenant farms to select a puppy. I discovered Juno has fathered a litter and is frequently there, so . . . ' He shrugged and she thought she detected sadness in his face. 'Anyway, there is no point in going now as you cannot keep a dog at Ravenscroft.' He drew back on the reins and prepared to turn the carriage.

She stared at him as if seeing him for the first time. His shoulders were slumped, his face pale. Whatever her feelings, she was suddenly convinced he truly wanted to marry her. Could her mother have been correct when she suggested he had been harbouring feelings for her since she was a girl?

Impulsively, she grabbed his arm. 'I have changed my mind. I would be fit for Bedlam if I turned down the most eligible bachelor in the kingdom. I also apologise for what I said. I neither dislike nor despise you. If I am totally honest, I have been coming to think of you more kindly these past few days.'

She had expected him to react with joy at her change of heart. Instead he merely glanced in her direction and nodded. 'Then we shall proceed as planned?'

'Yes, I will marry you in two weeks' time. However, I feel it only fair to tell you that if you had been agreeable, I would much prefer to have cancelled it. I promise I shall never mention this again; Mama did not love my father when they were married, but was soon content with her decision. Therefore I am hopeful I shall feel the same way eventually.'

Instead of being offended at her frankness, he laughed. 'Then I shall also speak openly. I wish to marry you because you are the only woman I've ever met who does not bore me. I'm not interested in love and all that flummery; that is best left to poets and silly young ladies. Far better to enter into a relationship with someone you find interesting and intelligent, some-one who will not become tiresome over the years.'

This was hardly a romantic speech but was exactly what she wanted to hear. Now she finally understood why he didn't want her to cancel the arrangement. She was well bred, pretty enough, and would not bother him with endless demands for new gowns and other fripperies.

'Then we are both satisfied. One thing we can be certain of, Sinclair: ours will not be a dull marriage. Every time we have been together lately, some calamity strikes.'

'I sincerely hope that this morning's misadventure means we are going to complete this mission without further nonsense. I cannot tell you how horrified my valet was when I appeared covered in dung.'

She giggled. 'My abigail was equally distressed — let us hope we can return home unsullied this time.'

He guided the horse expertly down a farm track and reined in beside a substantial wooden barn. She could hear puppies yapping inside. A young man in cord breeches and a flannel shirt came out to greet them. He touched his forelock. 'Good afternoon, Your Grace, miss. Glad you could make it. I reckon them puppies must know you're here. Just listen to the racket.' Although polite, this man showed no sign of subservience or of being in awe of the duke.

'I am so excited.' Lydia willingly took Sinclair's hand when he offered it. 'Are there many male puppies in the litter?'

'There are three bitches and four dogs, miss.' He grinned as he pulled open the door.

Lydia expected to be overrun by wriggling bodies, but the animals were contained in a pen. However, she was greeted by Juno, who had been in the pen with his progeny. 'Good heavens, what a clever boy you are, Juno. Please do not slobber on my coat.'

Sinclair snapped his fingers and immediately the enormous animal padded to his side and sat down. 'As you can see, these puppies are half wolfhound and half whatever Juno is. Have you spotted one you like?'

She bent over the barrier to examine the excited animals. Then she saw a lone puppy hiding in the far corner of the pen. This one was a sandy colour, with long ears and a mournful expression. 'If that puppy is a male then I want him.'

The men exchanged incredulous glances. Sinclair came to stand beside her. 'He is the runt of the litter. He might not even survive. Why not choose this fine fellow here? He looks exactly like his father.'

'No, my mind is made up. I will have no other. When can we collect him?'

The farmer scratched his head. 'I reckon as you could take him today, miss, if you want to.'

She smiled hopefully at Sinclair and he gave in to her plea. 'Very well, my dear. We will take him with us. This means that you must come to Stenning, for I doubt that puppy will remain in his box if you're not there to restrain him.'

The puppy was picked up and dropped unceremoniously into a waiting box. 'Please could I have a sack to put beneath him?' She was not thinking solely of his comfort, but of the likelihood of the dog being unable to control his bladder. Once the shivering puppy was securely wrapped in a sack he seemed happier. She scrambled onto the seat and held out her arms for the box. The duke shook his head.

'Move across, Miss Richmond. I shall hold this leaky individual and you will drive us back.'

Unable to argue with his logic, she did as he bid. 'Are you quite sure I am competent to return us in one piece?'

He settled back, one hand released the brake whilst the other scratched the puppy's ears. 'I am certain your injury will be no hindrance to our safety. Flick the whip and shake the reins a little. He is a well-trained gelding and will give you no trouble.'

Indeed that was the case, and she managed to drive them both without mishap to Stenning Hall. A groom and a stable boy were waiting for them. Sinclair handed the box to the stable boy. 'Joe, remember what I told you. This little scamp is in your sole charge for the next few weeks. It is your duty to house-train him and teach him his manners.

'I am sure he will be happy with you, Joe,' Lydia said. 'But I insist that you are kind and he must not be physically punished, whatever his misdemeanour.'

The urchin grinned at her. 'He'll come to no harm with me, Miss Richmond. Do he have a name yet?'

'Sandy is his name. Take care of him for me — he is a wedding gift from His Grace.'

On the return journey Sinclair took the ribbons. She sighed and touched his arm. 'Thank you for my gift. I like the gig, but Sandy will always be the best present I've ever had. Can I come over and see him every day until we are wed?'

His expression was innocent, but his eyes twinkled. 'Now you understand why I brought the puppy home today. If you are visiting Sandy then you cannot be getting up to mischief with Lady Alice.'

She tried to look offended. 'Whatever can you mean? Lady Alice and I are famous for our respectability and common sense.'

He laughed and squeezed her hand.

'That is doing it too brown, my dear. Your bosom friend is raising eyebrows with her behaviour. I sincerely hope she doesn't involve you in her entanglement with that cavalry officer.'

'Do you mean Captain Duvall? I have been introduced him and thought him a charming gentleman. He is not a fortune-hunter, for he has a small estate of his own as well as his stipend of an officer.' In the gloom she saw him raise a sceptical eyebrow. 'He is the youngest son of an earl, you know.'

They were drawing up outside Ravenscroft by then. 'Is that so? If you are correct, my love, then maybe my assessment is wrong. I shall make enquiries as to his status.' He reached out and touched her face with one finger. 'Will you give me your word not to become embroiled in any of Lady Alice's more outrageous schemes?'

'I promise. I think you are being overly cautious, Sinclair. Captain Duvall is as much in love with Alice as she is with him.'

'And her parents? Have they sanctioned the match?'

She shifted uncomfortably on the seat. 'I don't believe Alice has told them, but I'm sure Captain Duvall intends to speak to Lord Bellamy at her name-day ball.'

'Good grief! This is worse than I thought. I absolutely forbid you to become involved in what is likely to be the scandal of the century.'

She jumped down and moved a safe distance from him before replying. 'Alice is my friend. I know her, and she would not do anything untoward.' She curtsied and scampered up the stairs before he could call her back. She had no intention of following his high-handed demand. If Alice needed her help, she would be happy to give it.

13

Two weeks was scarcely enough time for Lydia to complete her wedding preparations. All her garments had to be carefully packed in tissue paper and transferred to Stenning. She also supervised the transfer of her most precious possessions: her books. Each time she accompanied the boxes.

'My dear girl, why have you brought books? My library here is extensive; you will have no need of yours.'

'I very much doubt, sir, that you have any recent novels. Anyway, these books are for my own apartment. They are not to go in the library.'

He strolled along with her to her rooms, pointing out his various ancestors portrayed in dark and gloomy paintings. 'I shall have your portrait taken as soon as we are married, Lydia. I'm sure you noticed the array of past duchesses as we came up the stairs just now.'

'I did, and none of them looked particularly delighted with their position.' She laughed and continued in this vein. 'Does your family have a history of unhappy marriages?'

Instead of laughing at her remark, he took her elbow and guided her to a secluded alcove halfway down the passageway. 'That is something I had meant to tell you, along with the reasons why you remain in ignorance of my being your guardian. Will you sit with me?'

Obediently, she took her position on the padded seat. She guessed she was not going to hear anything that would reassure her about this union.

He sat beside her, but didn't look in her direction, which was unusual. 'I know your comment was spoken in jest, sweetheart, but I am sorry to tell you your words were true. The Dukes of Stenning have an unfortunate propensity to select a duchess for the wrong reasons. I don't believe there's been a happy marriage in the last hundred years. The brides married for position and title, the dukes in order to produce an heir.' He paused as if collecting his thoughts. 'I think that is one of the reasons I have not considered marrying until now.'

'And what are the other reasons?'

'I did not expect to inherit the title so escaped into the army. Unfortunately my eldest brother died from the sweating fever and I was immediately recalled.' He sat back and faced her. He looked so sad and serious her heart went out to him. 'The next few years were difficult — my father and I did not get on.'

'And your mama?'

'I loved her dearly, but she died in childbirth when I was away from home. I did my best to protect my brothers from his excesses, but they were only safe from a beating when they were away at school.'

'Surely he did not beat you?' The

thought of someone as powerful as Sinclair submitting in this way did not sound likely.

'He would have liked to — but I would have floored him if he'd tried. When he died from an apoplexy five years ago I felt as if I had been released from prison. I have been busy ever since restoring the farms and cottages within our estates and ensuring my family wants for nothing.'

'I am sorry you had such a difficult time. Now, you are going to explain how you failed to inform us that you were the head of our household.'

By the time he had finished his story she had begun to understand him a little better. 'Although this is not a love match, we like and respect each other. I am not marrying you for position and you are not doing so in order to set up your nursery. I will be the first duchess who is happy to be part of the family.' She had started this sentence with the intention of cheering him up, but by the time she had completed it she

229

realised it was true.

'I sincerely hope that is the case, sweetheart. Do you know I am actually looking forward to saying my vows on Saturday? You are already a firm favourite with my family and the staff adore you. Which reminds me, Sandy has yet to be visited today. Do you still intend to go to the stables?'

She scrambled to her feet. 'Not today. I wish to see that my possessions have been correctly displayed.' They headed for her apartment, where Jenny was busy arranging books on a pretty walnut bookshelf. The girl immediately curtsied and vanished into the bedchamber.

'Already my rooms feel like home. I do appreciate that you have allowed me to bring my things — Mama tells me this is unusual in a husband.'

'I want you to be content, my dear. I frequently travel on business, so you will be alone here. I could not go away knowing you were uncomfortable.' He gestured at the freshly washed hangings. 'You can change all this if you wish. This apartment has not been refurbished since my mother died. The furniture is a trifle old-fashioned; I'm sure you will wish to order something more modern.' He grinned and looked years younger. 'However, I refuse to have anything with animal feet or with a Chinese or Egyptian theme.'

She pulled a face and shook her head. 'Oh dear, and I had my heart set on redecorating in red and gold and purchasing anything I could find that has serpents crawling over it.'

'Over my dead body, my girl. I can see I shall have to supervise your choices.'

'Well, I must say I am disappointed in you, Your Grace. You promised me I could order whatever I wanted and you have reneged on that already.'

'But think how much more fun it will be spending happy hours together every night looking in *Ackerman's Repository* and *La Belle Assemblée* for furniture and other fascinating things.'

She laughed and without thinking

gave him a playful push. Her hand was trapped by his. His heart was thundering beneath it. On glancing up she was caught by his intense stare. Slowly he raised her grubby hand to his lips and kissed each knuckle in turn. Her insides somersaulted and for some unaccountable reason her gown felt too tight.

Then he spun her around and moved her forward with a sharp smack on her bottom. 'You are going to run me ragged. I swear I shall have turned grey by Christmas.'

She rubbed her derriere and scowled at him. 'I believe I am learning your true colours, Sinclair. Am I to be brutalised as well as denied new furniture for my apartment?'

His expression changed from affectionate to horrified. 'I was teasing you. I apologise — '

She skipped away. 'There is no need. I, too, was funning. Now do go away, Sinclair. I have things to do before luncheon and I promised Mama I would be home for morning calls.'

When she arrived in the small dining room in which they served luncheon, she discovered he had been called away on estate business. Although she enjoyed the company of his sister and brothers, they did not engage her attention in the same way.

'Lady Margaret, my lords, pray excuse me as I wish to visit my puppy before I leave. Could you please tell His Grace that I shall not be coming tomorrow?'

The gentlemen stood up and bowed politely and the ladies smiled. Lady Margaret spoke for them. 'Of course you will not be here, Miss Richmond. There will be much to do the day before your wedding. I can assure you the wedding breakfast will be sumptuous and the chapel flower-filled.'

Lydia dipped and smiled. 'Thank you, my lady. I am sure it will be everything it should be. Will you be staying for the ball next week?'

'Indeed we will. My children are arriving tomorrow, as are many other family members. As the wedding is to be a small affair, we consider your shared ball to be the real celebration.' She nodded happily. 'I believe I can safely say that Lady Bellamy and I have arranged a spectacular event for next Saturday. There will be more than two hundred guests, a full orchestra and the most delicious supper. There will be cards for those who wish to play, and dancing for everyone else.'

'So many? I had not realised it would be so big.' Lydia hoped her dismay had not been noticed. 'I suppose that as there are two guest lists it was inevitable the ball would be well attended.' She curtsied a second time and hurried from the room. A footman was waiting to escort her to the stables, where Sandy greeted her with enthusiasm.

The stable boy in charge of his well-being tipped his cap and grinned. 'I reckon this little one is going to be a rare size. Just look at the size of his feet.'

Lydia dropped to her knees in the

straw. The puppy was on her lap, attempting to lick her face and wriggling in ecstasy as she tickled him. 'He has certainly grown apace since he's been here. He's beginning to recognise his name. Has he improved in his house training?'

The lad shook his head. 'I ain't getting on too well with that, Miss Richmond. I don't reckon His Grace will want the puppy in the house for a while yet.'

A groom poked his head over the half-door. 'Miss Richmond, your carriage is waiting to take you home.'

Immediately she scrambled up and shook the straw from her skirts. 'Be a good boy, Sandy. I shall see you in a few days.'

She was so busy with last-minute details that Lydia had no time to worry about how her life was going to change irrevocably on Saturday morning. That evening, as she was settling down to sleep, her mother drifted in.

'My darling, there are one or two

things I must tell you and I have put it off for far too long.'

'If you have come to explain to me my duties as a wife, there is no need. I am fully cognisant of what takes place in the marriage bed and have no wish to discuss it further.' This was not a complete lie; she had seen animals mating so had a rough idea of how things worked. What she did not know, and was quite happy to remain in ignorance of, was exactly what happened between a man and a woman. She sincerely hoped it would be a considerable time before she was obliged to discover this for herself.

'Thank goodness. I was rather dreading this talk. I suppose Lady Margaret has already given you all the information you need. I shall leave you to sleep, my dear. I must own that although I am happy for you, I am sad my beloved daughter will never sleep under my roof again.'

'Mama, I shall be living no more than half an hour away from you. We can see each other every day if we wish to, and anyway you and Uncle Edward will be married yourselves next year and going off on your travels.'

Her mother sniffed delicately and dabbed her eyes with a dainty handkerchief. 'I know that, but you are my only child and I feel as if I'm losing you tomorrow. Your husband to be is not the kind of gentlemen who will welcome over-frequent visits from his mother-in-law. I shall have to wait until I am invited, and you might not be able to come and go as you please.'

Lydia had a moment's misgiving on hearing this but quickly pushed it aside. 'I shall come and visit you whenever I wish, so even if you do not feel you can come to me, I shall come to you.' She threw back the covers and crawled across the bed to embrace her mother's shaking shoulders. 'Don't cry, Mama. You should be happy for me. I am sure that there are hundreds of young ladies who would love to be in my position. Papa would have been so proud of me.'

Her mother managed a watery smile and sniffed. 'I believe he must have intended this outcome all along, otherwise why would he have set the arrangement up?'

Eventually she was able to comfort her mother, who departed for her own bedchamber with her spirits restored. This left Lydia far too much time to dwell on what had been said, and it was several hours before she was able to fall asleep. When Jenny arrived with her morning chocolate, Lydia had had scarcely any sleep.

'I have no appetite this morning, thank you, Jenny, but am looking forward to a leisurely bath. I think that maybe I won't wear the emerald green after all. My other ensemble is also pressed and ready, is it not?'

Jenny was shocked by the suggestion. 'Oh no, miss, the green is perfect on you. With the bonnet freshly trimmed to match you will look a picture.'

Lydia was not convinced. When she had decided to defy convention by wearing such an unusual outfit she had not really considered the consequences. If she upset Sinclair on their wedding day, might this not be a bad omen? 'I shall take my bath and then try on each of the gowns. I won't decide until then. What time is it?'

'A little after seven o'clock, miss. You don't have to leave until half past ten — there's plenty of time.'

Four hours seemed remarkably little time. She could hardly credit she would soon become a duchess and the wife of a man not famous for his good humour and charm. Was she making a catastrophic error, or was she about to embark on a journey to happiness?

Her mother flitted in and out, offering advice and comfort as required. At last the time had come to choose the ensemble she was to wear for her wedding. She settled for the green sarcenet with the gold underskirt.

Jenny arranged her hair in a shiny coronet upon which the silk-lined bonnet fitted perfectly. Her accessories were gold, but the ribbons on her bonnet were emerald green to match her gown.

'You look like a princess in a storybook, miss. Ever so pretty. I'm sure His Grace will think you look beautiful.'

'I should not say so, but I agree with you. I have never looked better. Now, we just have to do up the buttons on my spencer and I am ready.' She glanced around the room that had been hers all her life. From today this would no longer be her home. She was about to gather up her skirts and leave for the last time when Jenny shrieked and called her back.

'Miss Richmond, you must wear your betrothal ring. His Grace will expect you to.'

The ring was so large it slipped easily over her soft kid gloves. She remembered to put it on her right hand and not the left. Another disaster averted at the last minute — the excitement made her forget her mother had yet to see her ensemble. Lydia arrived downstairs as the carriage pulled up outside. In the flurry of departure there was no time for her mother to comment. Once they were settled inside the vehicle, Lord Richmond was sitting opposite and Lydia heard his sharp intake of breath.

'My word, Lydia, that is not what I expected you to be wearing for your wedding day.'

'I am delighted to hear you say so, Uncle Edward. My intention was to surprise, and I seem to have succeeded admirably.' She waited for the storm of protest from her parent and when her mama remained silent, Lydia risked a glance in her direction. Her mother's face was averted and her shoulders shaking. 'Please don't cry, Mama. I can go back in and change. There is still time.' The only reply she got was a strangled gasp; she reached out to take her mother's hand.

'My darling girl, I love your ensemble. It is outrageous, courageous and exactly right for the occasion.' Only then did Lydia realise the shaking shoulders had been from laughter and not tears. 'There will be nobody in the chapel left in any doubt that you are the perfect match for the duke.'

These words drove out her fear. 'I sincerely hope he sees things in the same way as you, Mama. I want to show him I am not a child, but a woman grown with a mind of my own.'

Her uncle chuckled and bent forward and patted her on the knee. 'Then you have succeeded, my dear girl. I had my doubts about this union, but now I am sanguine you will make the perfect duchess.'

14

The Stenning family chapel was situated at the rear of the building and could only be accessed by walking through the entire length of Stenning Hall. Lydia, with her hand on her uncle's arm, was obliged to walk through rank upon rank of smiling, smartly dressed servants in order to reach her destination. She was so busy nodding at those who would soon be under her command that she had no time to be nervous.

'This establishment is enormous, my dear,' her mother said. 'Small wonder the duke has so many minions. I doubt you will be able to learn all their names.'

'Sinclair knows them all, so I shall endeavour to do the same. I have yet to visit the kitchen so I have no idea how many might be working there.' What a strange conversation to be having in the minutes before she pledged the rest of her life to a man she did not love.

'At last, we must be there. Did you observe the handsome flower arrangements along our route, Lydia?'

'I did, Mama. The duke's sister has gone to a great deal of trouble on my behalf.' No sooner had she spoken than she realised her mother might misinterpret this comment as a criticism at her lack of involvement. She pulled her arm from her uncle's and turned to face her mother, who was walking behind them. 'I wish we could have been married in the village church, but His Grace insisted we marry here.'

'Of course this is the correct venue. My love, you are causing a sensation. You must resume your progress.'

Lydia had forgotten they were being observed at this point by a row of uniformed footmen. Immediately she placed her hand back on Lord Richmond's arm and he led her towards the open doors of the chapel. This was far larger than she had expected, in fact bigger than the village church. There were stained glass windows, and all the trappings of a regular religious building.

The rousing music from the harpsichord encouraged the waiting guests to stand. Fifty or so fashionably dressed members of the aristocracy turned to look at her. Her confidence shrivelled under the combined gaze of so many haughty strangers. She wished she had worn her other choice and was not standing in front of so many accusatory faces wearing an unsuitable bright-green wedding gown.

Her uncle tried to move forward but her feet refused to budge. She was crushed. She wanted to run away and hide as she had always done when confronted with a problem. Her eyes were lowered and they stayed firmly on the floor; she wished it would open up and swallow her.

Then the duke was beside her. 'Sweetheart, I have come to walk you down the aisle myself. I swear you are the most beautiful and original bride in the country.' Her uncle stepped aside and the duke took her limp hand and threaded it through his arm.

Having him beside her restored her courage. She raised her head and looked at him. Instead of condemnation or resignation, she saw admiration, and something else she didn't recognise, in his expression. 'I should not have worn this — '

'You look perfect, my love. I could not have chosen you a more appropriate ensemble if I had tried. I shall have your portrait painted wearing it. Now, shall we be married, or are you intending to leave me standing at the altar?'

His words brought her to her senses. 'Why should I do that? If I hadn't wished to marry I would have stayed at home.' His eyes flashed and he covered her hand with his own. He bent his head and whispered in her ear.

'At this moment I wish we had decided to elope. I thank God there wasn't time for my sister to organise anything more elaborate. My knees are knocking. I would rather face battle than stand up in front of so many. Shall we get this over with, my love?'

'Fustian! You are no more frightened of saying your vows than I am.' She smiled at him, and he grinned back.

They marched briskly to the front and the service began. When the vicar blessed the ring she belatedly remembered she should not be wearing gloves. Sinclair understood immediately and removed the left one so smoothly she was certain no one in the congregation would have noticed her faux pas. Then he placed the ring on her finger and she was the Duchess of Stenning. She was fairly sure the custom was for the bride to be kissed by her new husband, but he didn't do so. She wasn't sure if she was disappointed or relieved.

'There, that wasn't so bad, was it? There is enough food prepared to feed twice as many guests as we have invited. I think we must lead the charge to the dining room.' He put his arm around her waist and guided her down the aisle and out to the passageway. His stream of inconsequential chatter allowed her no opportunity to reply, for which she was grateful. She found herself somewhat overwhelmed by everyone and everything.

He was walking too fast and she was obliged to trot in order to keep up. 'Sinclair, slow down. Our guests will think we are running away from them.'

In answer he lengthened his stride and then they were both running like children, leaving the congregation to follow as best they could. 'In here, we shall hide from them. They will be so busy devouring the mountains of food they will not notice the absence of the bride and groom.' He shouldered his way into a chamber and the door closed quietly behind them.

The room was gloomy and musty-smelling, the furniture shrouded in holland covers. 'Why are we in here?' Lydia asked.

'Hush, sweetheart. The stampede is passing by.' He drew her closer and she rested her head against his shoulder, trying to hold back her giggles. 'Here they come. They will be gone in a moment, and then we can come out of hiding.'

The corridor was silent and he pulled the door open a fraction. 'Excellent! Even the footmen have gone. Come along; I have a surprise for you.'

'Sinclair, we cannot abandon our own wedding breakfast. What will people think?'

'As I said before, I doubt they will notice. Don't worry; Margaret is privy to my plans and will make excuses for us if necessary.'

He took her hand and led her through a maze of passageways until they emerged at a side door. Outside, her gig was waiting and beside it stood a stable boy holding a wriggling puppy. 'In you get. Joe is coming with us. He can stand on the step with Sandy under one arm and still hold on.'

Where was he taking her? This was so exciting — far better than being questioned by his elderly relatives and found wanting in some way. 'Are we intending to join our guests at any point today?'

'Absolutely not! I have a house full of unwanted guests staying on until next Saturday in order to attend the celebration ball we are sharing with Lady Alice. I have no wish to spend any time with them when I can spend it getting to know my new wife.'

He flicked the whip and the gelding surged forward, almost dislodging the boy and the dog. Sinclair pushed the horse into a collected canter and the vehicle rattled over the stones and down a small paved track.

'Are we leaving the estate? I have nothing with me. My maid will be waiting for me in my apartment at Stenning Hall.'

The gig emerged from between the evergreen hedges and headed for a pretty stone-built house. 'Is this the Dower House?'

'No, my love. This is where my disreputable parent kept his mistress.'

She could not disguise her shock. 'Here? Right under your mother's nose? I can scarcely believe it.'

'Good God! Not when Mama was alive — he was a philanderer but not so lacking in decency as to have done such a thing. His first London ladybird was installed two years later; there followed a series of elegant and beautiful young women all eager to fleece my father of as much blunt as they could.'

Lydia wasn't sure how to take his motives for bringing her to little more than a house of ill repute. Did he consider her no better than the women who had resided here before her? The carriage halted. The front door stood open but there was no sign of any staff to assist them. Her pleasure in the adventure had been replaced by annoyance. If they had been in love and eager to share the experience of the marriage bed, then she could see the reason for abandoning their own celebration. But in the circumstances, this enterprise was inexplicable. The duke had not bothered to share his plans with her, and for all he knew she had been eagerly looking forward to being the centre of attention. Now, neither her uncle nor her mother would know where she was or why she and her new husband had vanished so abruptly.

Joe jumped down from the step and released the puppy, which immediately squatted and left a nasty pile just where Lydia was about to step down. This was too much. She sat up straight and glared at the duke. 'Take me back at once, Your Grace. I refuse to go inside this building. I am offended that you thought it permissible to bring me here when it was the home of the last duke's mistress.'

'Cut rope, Lydia. You are coming inside whether you like it or not.'

She stared stonily ahead and ignored him. She would not get down from the carriage under any circumstances. Without a by-your-leave, he scooped her up and stepped down from the gig before she could protest. 'Put me down this instant. I demand that you take me home.' He ignored her request and strode towards the open front door. Incensed beyond reason by his intransigence, she pulled his hair and grabbed his stock in order to strangle him.

He reeled to one side, painfully trapping her shoulder against the doorjamb. She tightened her grip on his neck cloth and yelled at him in a most unladylike way. 'You are a monster. You have no feelings, and if you don't put me down this instant you will regret it.'

He charged across a small entrance hall and into the drawing-room. There he released his hold and she tumbled to the floor, dragging him to his knees beside her as she refused to let go of his stock. His hands closed over her fingers and prised them open. She was spitting mad and launched herself at him and managed to land one resounding slap before he stopped her.

He held her at arm's length; his face was as red as hers. Her anger dissipated as suddenly as it had come. 'Are you done, my dear? I give you fair warning that if you slap me again I shall return the favour.' His tone was even, but his eyes were arctic, his nostrils pinched, and she knew he was barely containing his fury.

She gazed at the imprint of her hand across his face. Without thinking she reached out and placed her palm on his burning cheek. 'I have never struck another person in my life. That was unpardonable. I have no idea what happened or why I was so angry.'

His hand came up and covered hers, trapping it against his face. They were still sprawled on the floor, her back resting against a sofa, her skirts rucked up above her knees and her bonnet sitting crazily over one eye. His appearance was no better — his collar was torn, his neck cloth quite ruined, and three buttons were missing on his waistcoat.

'I believe I must blame your fiery temper on your hair, sweetheart. However, it was maladroit of me to tell you who the previous occupants of the house were. Small wonder you were furious. Did you think I had deliberately insulted you?'

'I did, and I still don't know what I'm doing here.' She supposed she should rearrange her skirts and get up from the floor, but her limbs were leaden and she had not the energy to do so. She flopped back, pushing the bonnet further over her face.

Then his fingers tenderly untied the bow and removed it. 'There, that's a great improvement. Now, allow me to restore you to your feet and show you why I brought you here.'

Wearily, Lydia held out her hand and he pulled her upright. She no longer cared why they were here; between them they had ruined what should have been a special day and a family celebration. What poor Mama would think did not bear considering — but her life was no longer her mother's business. Her husband would do as he pleased and there was no one that could stop him.

She had not the energy to speak. She must endure whatever he had planned without complaint. She had behaved like a vicious shrew and deserved to be miserable. He guided her through the drawing-room and then paused at open double doors. 'This is why we are here. I thought my surprise would please you.'

She raised her head and was obliged to clutch his arm. 'You did this for me, and I repay you by behaving like a fish-wife.'

Set out in a south-facing, empty, glass-fronted room was a picnic — two enormous hampers stood waiting to be opened, rugs and cushions were spread invitingly on the tiled floor, and scampering towards Lydia was her puppy. As she bent down to welcome

Sandy she had time to see that piled along the wide window seat were books, painting materials and a bat and ball; pressed up against the wall was a pianoforte with a double piano stool and a substantial stack of music.

The little dog wriggled and his long pink tongue licked away her tears. Then the trickle became a flood and she couldn't hold back a sob. The duke removed the puppy and shooed him away.

'Darling, please don't cry. I wanted to make this day something you would never forget — a day of fun and happiness, not regret. I hoped I might persuade you our marriage could be successful if given a chance.'

She flung herself into his waiting arms and they closed around her. He stroked her back and murmured affectionately until she was done. Eventually she gulped and mopped her face with a large white square he had helpfully pushed into her hand. She was still unable to speak; her emotional outburst had left her drained.

'No, little one, don't try and get up. Let me take you to the cushions where we can be comfortable.'

She relaxed into his embrace and he regained his feet as if it was the most usual thing in the world to be carrying his wife about the place. She sniffed and rubbed her cheeks with the mangled end of his stock. The handkerchief was already sodden. Sandy was yapping around his ankles in excitement and he swore at him.

'Sinclair, your language is more suited to the barrack room than the abode of the Duke of Stenning.'

He chuckled and his arms tightened. 'Perhaps you do not know that I was once an officer in the army. I fear I am forever tainted by this association.'

With her still in his arms, he knelt and placed her gently amongst the piled cushions. She kept hold of his hand, forcing him to sit beside her. 'You have succeeded in your plans; I shall never forget today. I behaved appallingly and you have been the perfect gentleman throughout. I do not deserve to be treated so kindly.' She gestured around the room and smiled at him. 'You have brought together four things that I love: picnic, painting, piano and puppy.' She counted them out on her fingers and wished with all her heart that her mother had told her the secret and that she had not ruined his kind gesture. 'You have done all this for me, to make my day special, and I have done my best to ruin it. And, to make matters worse, I have done nothing for you.'

He had not released her hand during this speech. In fact, he was staring at her in a way that made her feel hot and bothered. 'There is one thing you could do for me right now that will make today perfect for me.'

'Anything. I will do anything to make up for my — '

'Wait, sweetheart, before you make a promise you cannot keep.' His expression was watchful, no longer confident of success.

Lydia swallowed nervously. She knew what he wanted from her and was not sure she could give it to him, even though she owed him everything. She closed her eyes, took a deep breath, and sat up straight. He wanted her to become his true wife. He had the right to insist, but he was asking her permission and if she refused he would never force the issue.

'I don't care what it is you want of me. I am your wife and I will fulfil my duty if that is what you want.'

'God's teeth! I want to kiss you, not take you to bed.' He sounded so horrified that an inappropriate bubble of laughter escaped.

She scrambled to her knees and attempted to throw herself into his arms. 'I should be offended, sir, at your reluctance to make me your true wife, but I'm more than happy to be kissed. In fact, I absolutely insist that you do so immediately.'

15

This time Lydia was ready for the unpleasant sensation of a man's mouth covering hers. She was determined not to recoil or overreact as she had done previously. He responded to her precipitous action not by immediately kissing her, but by holding her at arm's length. 'I wish to seal our union with the traditional kiss — no more than that. I thought you would prefer it not to take place in full view of the congregation.' He examined her face as if searching for a clue to her innermost thoughts. She held her breath, not sure if she was eager or dreading the experience. He nodded as if satisfied by what he saw revealed. Slowly he drew her closer until his breath warmed her cheek. 'Look at me, sweetheart. I want to see your lovely face.'

She opened her eyes to discover he was inches from her. Close to, his eyes were not pure blue, but flecked with gold and grey. The stubble on his chin and upper lip was as dark as his hair. His teeth were even, no sign of decay or damage. Her head swam as she inhaled his heady, masculine scent — a mix of lemon, leather and something she didn't recognise.

He closed the gap, first cupping her face with one hand, and then his firm lips touched hers, sending a shock wave of heat racing around her body. Nothing had prepared her for this. She had expected to be repulsed, but instead she wanted more from him, to be crushed against his chest as had happened last time.

His mouth moved softly across hers, then travelled down along her jawline, leaving behind a trail of exquisite sensation. Somehow her hands found their way around his neck and buried themselves into the short crisp hair above his collar, pulling him closer, demanding he kiss her more thoroughly.

He raised his head and the intensity of his gaze inflamed her already overheated skin. Finding the answer he wanted reflected in her face, he lowered his head, and this time his kiss demanded a response. Several deeply satisfying minutes later, he released her with what sounded like a sigh of regret.

'Enough, my love. Much as I would like to take things further, I have given you my word and have no intention of breaking my promise any time soon.'

She was strangely restless, as if something momentous had almost happened. 'I had not expected to enjoy the experience. However, I am obliged to admit kissing you is actually quite enjoyable.'

What he had been going to say was cut short as a small furry body insinuated itself between them, nipping and licking in turn. 'Sandy, stop that at once. Bad dog. You must not bite.' Lydia held out the wriggling puppy not a moment too soon as a thin stream of yellow liquid shot from him. She dropped him with a squeal of horror.

'Horrible animal! I'm beginning to regret you included him in our picnic.'

The puppy, unbothered by his reprehensible behaviour, scampered off to chase a sunbeam on the far side of the room.

'I am eager to discover what has been packed in our hampers,' Lydia said. 'Are we to serve ourselves today?'

'It will give us time to get to know each other a little better. However, both your maid and my valet are upstairs somewhere and there are sufficient indoor servants to look after us, but not to intrude in any way.'

'In which case, pray excuse me for a short time. I want to change into something more comfortable, especially as you wish me to wear this gown in my portrait.'

'Then I shall do the same.' He smiled wryly. 'God knows what my man will say when he sees me in tatters.'

'I expect he has become resigned — I know that Jenny fully expects to see me in disarray every time I return from your company.'

He took her hand and pulled her upright. 'There is champagne and lemonade in one of the hampers, but I think I would prefer coffee. Shall I order some chocolate for you?'

'Coffee will be perfect, thank you. I hope Sandy does not get into the food baskets in our absence.' She shivered as the sun disappeared behind a bank grey cloud. 'Perhaps you could ask for a fire to be lit as well?'

Her bedroom was facing east and had a view of the sea. There was no private sitting-room, but it did have a small dressing room and closet where she discovered Jenny putting away clothes.

'I wish to change from my wedding gown into something warm and comfortable. I sincerely hope you packed a suitable outfit.'

Jenny curtsied. 'Yes, Your Grace. I

265

have your russet gown. I believe that will be perfect.'

Being addressed so formally made Lydia uncomfortable, but things had changed and she supposed she was expected to treat the staff differently now she was a duchess. 'Thank you. I must not be long; I promised to be back within a quarter of an hour.'

She was on her way downstairs in slightly less than that but her husband was already waiting for her. He was leaning nonchalantly against the wall as if he had been there for some time. He had changed into a dark blue topcoat, another white shirt and an extraordinarily bright waistcoat. This cravat was tied casually, but his boots, as always, were polished to a high shine.

She intended to compliment him on being so speedy but said something else entirely. 'That is a very bright waistcoat, Sinclair. Not at all your usual style.'

'Splendid, isn't it? My youngest brother, Harry, had it made for me last Christmas. He said I was a dull dog and

needed to wear something more cheer-
ful.'

'He is the . . . err . . . flamboyant
young gentleman you introduced me to
last week?'

'The macaroni — his collar points
are so high he can barely turn his head.
He wears the most appalling waistcoats,
but no doubt he will grow out of it in
time.' He patted his chest and grinned.
'As you can imagine, I have never worn
this item until now. I thought today was
the ideal occasion to appear in something colourful.'

'I expect I shall get used to it. Can
you imagine the reaction of your elderly
relatives if you appeared dressed as you
are?'

Laughing together, they hurried back
to the garden room, which was already
considerably warmer as a huge apple
log fire was burning merrily. The
pungent aroma of coffee filled the
space. An enormous silver pot was
waiting for them on a low side table
beside the hampers.

'Good heavens, Sandy's little accidents have been removed,' Lydia observed.

'The puppy has also been removed; I expect Joe was summoned to look after him. Much as I like him, a leaky puppy is not conducive to a relaxing picnic.'

By the time the hampers were empty, the coffee, lemonade and champagne drunk, darkness had fallen outside and Lydia had lit the dozen candles left on the mantel shelf. She had played several of the tunes from the music sheets, they had sung together and played a lively game of spillikins. When she yawned for the third time, Aubrey laughed.

'I think it's time for you to retire. You have been half asleep for the past hour or so.'

'I didn't sleep at all well last night, and I believe the champagne has gone to my head. I do hope Cook was not preparing us an elaborate dinner, as I couldn't eat another morsel.'

'No, you are free to go to your room without feeling guilty that you are abandoning me to a lonely meal on my wedding day.' He sighed dramatically and clutched his chest.

'You are an idiot, sir. If I had known I was to marry a simpleton with a disastrous taste in waistcoats, I might have reconsidered.' She put her hands on her hips and attempted to look fierce. 'If you appear in that monstrosity tomorrow I will not speak to you. Even such a top-lofty gentleman as yourself cannot wear puce, purple and yellow stripes without looking a figure of fun.'

'And you, my angel, are an impudent baggage. I have never been so insulted in my life.' He folded his arms and stared down his aristocratic nose, but his eyes were dancing with mischief. 'I am going to demand a forfeit for your temerity.' He moved so quickly she had no time to evade him. Her feet left the ground as he held her above his head like a trophy.

'Put me down this instant.' When he showed no sign of obeying her she tried another tack. She gulped. 'Oh dear! I fear I am going to cast my accounts.'

'Really? I shall find you a suitable receptacle, my love. Never fear, I will be here to hold your head as you vomit.' He lowered her so she was held against his chest and then strolled across the room as if actually looking for a container.

'You are impossible. Will you put me down if I apologise?' She thought it better not to pummel his chest, even in fun. She had no wish to be slapped in return.

He stopped his perambulations and smiled into her eyes. 'I shall release you for another kiss.'

By the time he put her down she was feeling decidedly hot and bothered. Why was it that kissing him raised her temperature in this way? He kept hold of her hand and for some reason she didn't wish to remove it. Having spent a companionable few hours in his company, she no longer thought of him as a distant stranger.

At the bottom of the stairs he let go

of her hand. 'Good night, sweetheart. I would like to ride with you tomorrow. Can you be ready at first light? Or do you prefer the breakfast before you go out?'

'Ride then eat will suit me perfectly. Good night, Sinclair — '

'No, I refuse to be addressed any longer as Sinclair. Can you not bring yourself to call me by my given name? We are so beyond the pale I cannot believe such a small breach of etiquette will harm our reputations further.'

'You have been Your Grace, or sir, ever since I've known you. It will be hard to use your given name — but I will promise I will try.' She stepped away and curtsied. 'I bid you good night, Aubrey. I look forward to seeing you in the morning. And thank you for a delightful day.'

He bowed low. 'I have also enjoyed today; in fact, I cannot remember having spent such a happy time before. I think that bodes well for the future together, don't you think?'

'I do. I'm sure we will have frequent furious arguments and misunderstandings, and no doubt we must expect a catastrophe a week. But if we continue as we have done then neither of us will regret our decision.'

★ ★ ★

The next few days were spent riding, reading, talking and dining together. They had no visitors and wished for none. On Saturday, the morning of the grand ball, Lydia left the small house wishing they could remain there indefinitely. The duke — no, she must call him Aubrey now even in her thoughts — had proved himself a charming and delightful companion. The arrogant aristocrat she had come to dislike over the past two years was a different person entirely, and one she hoped would not return when he resumed his position as the Duke of Stenning.

Over the past week she had become

accustomed to her new role and was able to nod and smile at the servants as she walked past in the same nonchalant manner that her husband did. It seemed strange walking for the first time to her new apartment. She wondered what Aubrey's rooms were like; a tiny shiver of excitement shook her at the thought that sometime in the future she would see them for herself. She wished now that she had allowed her mother to talk to her on this subject as she still didn't know exactly what happened in order to conceive a child, or even if the husband visited the wife in her own room or the other way round.

It was going to take her some time to become accustomed to footmen opening and shutting doors for her. At least she knew her way to her rooms, and how to find the main hall and drawing room. However, she had no idea where she should go to eat her breakfast tomorrow, but assumed one of the many indoor staff could direct her.

When she stepped into her sitting room she found not just her own abigail waiting for her, but two other young women as well. Jenny curtsied. 'Your Grace, welcome home. This is Sally and this Mary. They will be assisting me in your care.' The girls bobbed, but neither met her eyes.

'Thank you, Jenny. I'm sure we will all get along famously. As we are to dine at five o'clock and it is already afternoon, I think I had better take my bath and wash my hair immediately.'

'We had words that you were on your way, Your Grace, and your bath is waiting in the anteroom. I have added rose essence to the water. I hope that is acceptable.'

Jenny sounded like a stranger, not a girl Lydia had grown up with and considered almost a friend. She was surrounded by polite, friendly strangers. Apart from her husband (she was beginning to enjoy thinking of him as that), she now had nobody to talk to. She doubted Alice would be a frequent visitor — her friend was a little afraid of the duke.

After a relaxing bath, she sat comfortably on a low stool in front of the roaring fire in her bedroom whilst Jenny brushed her hair dry. The mantel clock struck three. 'Goodness, is that the time already? I must be downstairs half an hour before Lady Alice and her family and guests arrive.'

'Your hair is done, Your Grace. If you would care to step into your chemise and petticoats I shall dress it for you.'

'I thought I would wear the emeralds that my grandmother left me. Can you arrange my hair so the tiara is shown off to best advantage?'

As Lydia sat in front of the glass she detected an atmosphere of excitement amongst the three girls. There was something she didn't know that they did. Her lips curved. She would not ask. She was certain Aubrey had a hand in this and whatever he had arranged, she would be pleased with it.

At four o'clock her hair was done, her

silk stockings tied securely and her soft lawn petticoat laced. All she had to do was put on her ball gown and add the emerald ear bobs and necklace.

'If you would care to stand in the centre of the room, Your Grace, we will drop the gown over your head.' Jenny nodded to her assistants and they vanished into the cavernous closet. Lydia stood up and waited expectantly. For some reason the girls didn't reappear immediately. Was something wrong with her gown? She had never worn this item, and had been saving it especially for Lady Alice's ball.

There was a rustle behind her and she raised her arms. Silk slithered across her overheated skin and settled around her ankles. Startled, she opened her eyes and her knees all but gave out. This was not the new gown she was expecting. It was a dress she had never seen before. The underskirt was emerald green, and over it floated the lightest, palest gold spangle she had ever seen. Her eyes filled and her throat clogged with tears. Aubrey had somehow arranged for this beautiful confection to be made after he had seen her wedding gown.

'Here, madam, are the matching slippers. There is also a wrap, fan and reticule to complete the ensemble. His Grace does not want you to wear gloves tonight.'

The evening slippers were tiny, exquisite bugle beads sewn on in flower patterns to match the sleeve edges and décolletage. A slight noise behind Lydia made her look up and she met the eyes of her husband in the mirror.

'You look *ravisante*, my love. Exactly as I imagined you would in that gown. Turn round and let me fasten your necklace.' Jenny handed it to him and when his hands brushed her neck she experienced that same tingle of expectation. 'Now, tilt your head and I will put in your earrings.' There was a slight tug as each was inserted and then, instead of stepping away, he rested his hands on her shoulders and turned her around.

She finally found the breath to speak. 'Thank you so much. This is the most beautiful ball gown any girl could have. I cannot believe you did this for me. I feel like a fairy princess.'

He pressed cool lips on hers. 'Give me your left hand, darling.' He dipped into his waistcoat pocket and removed a small velvet box held together with intricate gold filigree. He flipped it open, removed the ring and tossed the box aside. Then a stunning square-cut emerald surrounded with diamonds was pushed over her knuckle to rest snugly against her wedding band.

'I noticed the family ring was too big for you, and I decided to have another made instead. Lady Richmond showed me your emeralds and I had my jeweller make something to complement your parure.'

Lydia held her hand out to examine it more closely. 'I love it. I could not have chosen anything better.' She wanted to fling her arms around him and express her gratitude, but the sound of people going past warned her they were in danger of being tardy. 'I cannot thank you properly now. I promise I shall do so later.'

His eyes darkened and held her captive by their intensity. He slid her arm through his, and when she was close enough, he whispered in her ear. 'I shall hold you to that, sweetheart. I am the most fortunate man in the kingdom tonight. I have never seen you look more beautiful.'

16

The resident guests were already milling about in the grand drawing room, sipping sweet sherry wine or champagne. The butler stood guard at the front door, flanked by a row of maids and footmen. They were awaiting the arrival of Lady Alice, her family and their guests.

'Do we wait here to greet the Bellamys?' Lydia asked Aubrey.

'No, they are joint hosts of this occasion, so it would not be appropriate. Would you like to see the ball room?' She nodded and he led her down the spacious corridor to the open double doors at the far end. 'I should have given you a conducted tour of your new home, sweetheart, but what with one thing and another it quite slipped my mind.'

'I would be better served with a map

of this establishment — I swear I've walked around it several times and never been in the same place twice.' She gazed around the huge room in delight. 'Lady Margaret has excelled herself. How clever to have divided the room in this way, with one end celebrating Lady Alice's birthday and the other our wedding. Having white flowers and ribbons for us and pink for Alice is exactly right.' She walked into the centre of the room in order to examine the portraits that took pride of place on each end wall.

'Do you like the painting of ourselves? The artist was summoned from London and will remain to paint your portrait next week.'

'I cannot imagine how he achieved two paintings in so short a time.' She stood underneath the one depicting herself and Aubrey. 'I see now that it has been done in watercolour. The likeness is remarkable — I wonder where he got mine from, as I haven't sat for him before.'

'Don't you recognise the image? It is from your own self-portrait that Lady Richmond supplied from your portfolio.'

'Good heavens! So it is — no wonder it is so flattering. How fortunate the gallery in which the musicians will play is situated in the centre of the far wall. Now no one can say they are favouring Alice or ourselves.'

As Aubrey and she strolled back hand-in-hand to the vast vestibule, she recalled his suggestion that they should appear to be besotted with each other. Her heart flipped. They had no need to pretend — for some reason they were both acting as if it were true.

There was no time to dwell on this extraordinary idea, as the next half hour was spent in greeting the new arrivals. Alice embraced her.

'Lydia, you look so lovely. I am green with envy over your gown — there will not be another like it here. You look radiant; I do believe that married life is to your taste after all.'

'I am surprisingly content. Thank you for your compliments. My husband gave me this gown as part of my wedding gift. You look beautiful in your rose-pink silk. I'm so glad Lady Bellamy agreed you could wear it and not oblige you to wear white as is customary for debutantes.' There was a light touch on her shoulder and she glanced round and smiled.

'Dinner is about to be announced, sweetheart. As we must lead our guests in, we should make our way to the doors to the dining room.' He nodded at Alice and then placed Lydia's hand on his arm.

'I understand we should be first, but how will everybody else know where they should be placed?'

He chuckled. 'I can assure you if anyone is incorrectly positioned there will be someone there to set them straight. At least tonight we can sit together at one end of the table instead of being separated by many yards of mahogany. Lady Alice and her parents will be sitting at the other end, her guests and family on her left, and our guests and family on my left.'

'The grand dining room is another room I've not inspected. There must be over one hundred people here; it is hard to imagine a table long enough to accommodate us all.'

It took a considerable time to seat everyone, and even longer for the dozens of courses and removes to be eaten. Voices got louder and laughter more raucous as the evening progressed. Lydia picked at her food. She was finding being the centre of attention rather overwhelming. 'Do I have to take the ladies away so you can drink port?' she asked Aubrey.

'Not tonight. This wretched meal has gone on for so long that the rest of our guests will be arriving imminently.' He snapped his fingers and the butler appeared at his shoulder. 'Inform Lady Bellamy dinner is over.'

Lydia glanced down the table and saw that at least half the diners were still eating dessert; the fruit and marchpane fancies were standing on the sideboard waiting to be served. Surely it was bad manners to expect people to leave their meal so abruptly? She was about to say so when her husband tossed his napkin aside and stood up, frowning at her when she did not immediately follow suit. To her astonishment, Lord and Lady Bellamy did the same at the far end of the table, leaving their guests little option.

Footmen moved the chairs aside and Aubrey escorted her from the doors behind them as the Bellamys exited through their door. No doubt everyone else would follow on behind. This time they were to form a welcome line; she and Aubrey first and Lord and Lady Bellamy and Alice beside them. Those invited to the ball were announced loudly, then they filed past, offering congratulations and good wishes to both parties. The cavalry officers in their scarlet regimental stood out among the black-garbed gentlemen.

Captain Duvall had looked particularly dashing. This procedure went remarkably smoothly and by half past ten the vestibule was all but empty.

Aubrey bowed politely to the Bellamys and guided Lydia down the flower-lined passageway to the ballroom, which was now humming with conversation.

'The last time I danced with you, Lydia, I trod on your gown. I promise that will not happen tonight. I have asked for a waltz to be played first and we shall lead the dancing.'

'What about Alice? She cannot waltz.'

'The second dance will be a country dance. She will lead that one and we shall not participate.'

The orchestra struck up a chord and the master of ceremonies announced the dance. Aubrey led Lydia to the centre of the ballroom. To her horror, no one else joined them. 'I cannot dance with so many people watching me — I'm sure to tread on your toes and embarrass us both.'

'You will do no such thing. I am going to hold you indecently close. We will scandalise the tabbies, but that way I can ensure you do not miss your step.'

The music began and he swept her away. He danced superbly and she was able to follow his lead with no difficulty. They whirled from one end of the ballroom to the other. She was floating, her feet scarcely touched the ground. She forgot where she was, who she was, and gave herself up to the most magical experience of her life.

Then other couples began to join them on the floor and they were obliged to travel more slowly in order not to collide with them. Aubrey's smile made her toes curl in her slippers. 'Tonight, my love, you are every inch my duchess.' She was overcome with emotion at his praise — but then he continued, 'But tomorrow, no doubt, you will revert to being a headstrong, outrageous young hoyden.'

She tilted her head and glared at him.

'And no doubt tomorrow you will revert to being an arrogant, dictatorial aristocrat.'

'That's better, my dear. I was becoming a trifle unnerved by your docility.' He expertly manoeuvred past two couples, off the floor and into the spacious corridor that ran alongside. The orchestra was clearly audible and he grinned at her, dropped his arm, and she was literally dancing on air. She hastily put both hands around his neck and clung on. He eventually stopped, leaning against the panelled wall, his chest heaving and his eyes filled with a wicked glint.

'Well, that was certainly invigorating. Did you enjoy your first waltz, my angel?' He slackened his grip and she slid down his front. Her knees buckled and she sat with a thump, surrounded by a sea of green and gold.

She wasn't sure whether to be furious or entertained by his behaviour. 'Don't stand there sniggering, sir. Help me up. I'm terrified of treading on my skirts and tearing my gown.' She smiled sweetly. 'You might recall you have already ruined one ball gown.'

He reached down and held her in the air; then with a commendably straight face, he shook her from side to side. 'What are you doing? Put me down at once.'

'I am merely ensuring your divine ensemble has no creases.'

Why was he being so annoying? The music finished and people clapped. They would be joined in a minute by others wishing to stretch their legs in the cooler atmosphere of the passage. She would not let him get away with his nonsense. She stretched out and took the end of his intricately tied neck cloth and gave it a hefty pull. As she expected it unravelled, leaving him no longer the smartest gentleman at the ball.

She was running down the passage before he could react, and as she skidded in an unladylike manner, around the corner she came face-to-face with Alice. Her friend was in tears.

'Quickly, Alice, come upstairs with me where we can be private. You must not be seen like this.'

Thankfully neither Jenny nor the girls were around — they had been drafted to help in the ladies' retiring rooms, which were downstairs.

'Lydia, Adam spoke to Papa just now. He asked for my hand and Papa sent him away and threatened to have him cashiered for having the effrontery to speak to me first.'

'How did Lord Bellamy know about you and Captain Duvall? Surely he didn't mention he had been seeing you in secret?'

'Of course he didn't. But Papa told him I would not be interested as I had no wish to be married. Adam was obliged to tell him that we were in love.'

'Small wonder your father threatened to report him to his commanding officer. How could the captain be so stupid as to have mentioned it? Are you quite sure he is the man you want to marry?'

Alice sobbed noisily and Lydia handed her a handkerchief. 'How can you say that to me? I thought you would understand. You are my best friend and know what it is to be in love.'

'I wish it were true. The duke and I are merely friends. We decided to play-act tonight to make everyone believe we married so quickly because we are desperately in love. We obviously succeeded.'

Alice blew her nose and wiped her eyes. 'I never heard such nonsense in my life. Only a man in love would arrange so many surprises and gifts for his wife. That was no act, at least on his part.'

'I sincerely hope that you are mistaken. I have just deliberately ruined his appearance. He will be hopping mad with me now. What are you going to do? Is Captain Duvall intending to try again when Lord Bellamy has got used to the idea?'

'I don't know. Papa had him escorted

from the house and I had no time to talk to him. What am I going to do? He is everything I've ever wanted in a husband and I am determined not to give him up.'

'Lord Bellamy has never denied you anything. I expect when he has calmed down he will realise how much you love Captain Duvall and will agree, at least, to let you see him.'

'Do you think so? I shall go and speak to him — '

'No, not tonight. That would be a disaster. You must go downstairs and pretend to enjoy the rest of your birthday ball.' She glanced at the clock. 'Botheration! We must return to the ballroom immediately, for there is going to be a toast for each of us in a quarter of an hour.'

She waited whilst her friend washed her face and tidied her appearance, and then the two of them strolled back down the stairs as if they had been doing nothing more unusual than spending time together. There was no sign of either Lord or Lady Bellamy or her husband. Was he in his apartment looking for a fresh cravat?

'Lady Alice, Your Grace, you are awaited in the ball room.' The butler bowed low and Lydia nodded and drew her friend along the passageway towards the hum of activity.

'My dear, I was about to send out a search party. Lady Alice, your parents are becoming anxious. Perhaps you would care to join them?' The duke smiled at Alice and winked at Lydia. He patted his immaculate stock and captured her hand in his. 'Come along; we must be congratulated together, and then I suppose we must dance again.' He sounded so miserable at the prospect that she giggled, and his lopsided grin sent an unbecoming flush from her toes to her crown.

Champagne was handed round and the master of ceremonies called for a toast in their honour, and then the same was done for Alice. 'Do you mind very much if I spend some time with my mother? I have not spoken to her since the wedding.'

'If you are quite sure you don't require me to stand up with you, I shall escape to the billiard room for an hour or so. There is to be another waltz before supper and I shall be back to claim that dance.'

'Where do you wish me to wait? You will never find me in this crush.'

He raised her hand to his lips and kissed it. 'I will always find you, my love.' This romantic speech and his kiss made her wonder if there was a faint possibility Alice had been right. Then he spoilt the moment. 'I am a head taller than most of the people here and you are wearing the most spectacular gown — these two things make your whereabouts easy for me to discern.'

'Not if I am standing behind a pillar,' she replied pertly.

His unexpected laugh caused several heads to turn in astonishment. The duke was not famous for his sense of fun. '*Touché*, sweetheart. I shall see you in an hour or so.'

Her mother and uncle were overjoyed to see her and, like Alice, believed the union was blissfully happy. Lydia did not have the heart to tell them otherwise. If her mother knew the true state of affairs she might put off her own plans for matrimony and travel and that would never do.

'Your uncle and I are going to take to the floor for the supper dance, my love. Look, your husband is coming to claim you. We are to sit together for supper. I'm hoping there will be no obstacles to that tonight. We have yet to sit down together as a family. Mind you, I have spoken since to Lady Margaret and find her a delightful person.'

The ball continued unabated until two in the morning, when the carriages were called for. Lydia was exhausted and more than ready to retire to the quiet of her own apartment. This would be her first night sleeping in her new home and she was rather looking forward to it. She decided to slip away.

Amid the general fuss surrounding the departure of the guests, no one would notice the disappearance of the hostess. Alice and her family had departed some time ago, apparently in perfect harmony.

Jenny had been released from her duties downstairs and was waiting to help her disrobe. The fairy-tale gown was taken to be sponged and pressed, the spectacular emeralds safely restored to their boxes. Lydia was in her chemise when there was a sharp knock on her bed chamber door. She froze.

'See who it is, Jenny.' Before her maid reached the door, it opened and her husband strode in. He gestured abruptly and her maid vanished, leaving them alone.

Her stomach squeezed and her hands were clammy. There could be only one reason why he had come to her room and she was not ready for that.

'We will remember, my love, that you owe me a favour. I have come to claim it now.'

17

Lydia forced her lips to curve in a semblance of a smile and perched on the end of the bed, hoping she looked less terrified than she was. He was still fully clothed — surely a husband would not come to his wife like this if he intended to share her bed? Her breathing steadied and her smile became genuine.

'I do hope whatever it is, Aubrey, that it will not take too long, for as you can see I am about to retire.'

His eyes widened and an almost predatory expression replaced his amusement. Then he grinned and pointed to her hair. 'I wish to release your hair. I have yet to see it unbound and I am determined not to wait another minute for that pleasure.' He moved slowly towards her and she couldn't look away. 'No, let me do it for you.'

She closed her eyes and gripped the

comforter in the hope this would disguise her trembling. He was so close that his familiar smell filled her nostrils. The bed dipped as he settled beside her. Then his hands were sliding through her hair, seeking the pins that held it secure. As each one was removed, he caressed her scalp and her nervousness was replaced by something she didn't recognise.

Her hair tumbled around her shoulders and he buried his hands in it, smoothing out the tangles with his fingers. 'Magnificent. Everything I . . . I expected it to be.' His voice was gruff as if he was in pain, then the bed shifted and he was gone. The door closed softly behind him, leaving her strangely restless and not quite sure what had happened between them.

She called but Jenny did not return. Her maid must think that Aubrey had come to demand his marital rights and had made herself scarce until the morning. Lydia pulled her chemise over her head and replaced it with her nightgown. As the voluminous folds of embroidered cotton settled around her, she couldn't help thinking what an unglamorous garment this was for a new bride. Her cheeks pink, she scrambled into bed, determined to send for the local seamstress and have some more attractive garments made up.

She slept late the next morning and by the time she descended several of the guests were preparing to depart. She stood by her husband in the hall to bid them farewell. Eventually he draped his arm around her shoulders and squeezed her affectionately.

'They were the last, my dear. We finally have the house to ourselves. Are you hungry? I am famished. I have arranged for a light repast to be served in the butterfly drawing room.'

'I cannot see why you are complaining, sir, as we were absent for the entire week they were here. I have not seen this drawing room, but then there must be a thousand rooms in this establishment.'

'I think at the last count there were one hundred and thirty-three.'

She smiled saucily. 'How extraordinary! I am living in a house that magically grows under its own volition.'

'Don't bandy words with me, madam. I am sharp set and in no mood for your nonsense.'

'I do apologise, Your Grace. I shall keep my nonsense until after you have eaten.'

He chuckled and his hand brushed her face. 'I am working on your map, sweetheart. I thought it an excellent notion. I fear that many a guest has perished wandering the empty corridors, unable to find their way to sustenance.'

In complete accord they strolled past the grand dining room, turning right and two footmen jumped to attention and opened the doors to the room they were seeking.

'What a pretty chamber. I can see why it is so named. Who painted the butterflies around the walls? They are exquisite and not at all familiar.'

'One of the many disenchanted duchesses did it many years ago. I was told she had a yearning to travel and as she could not do so, she painted what she might have seen instead.'

A buffet lunch had been set out for them on the sideboard but, as at the picnic, they were to serve themselves. When they had finished, Aubrey suggested they take the tour of the building together and Lydia acquiesced. This occupied the rest of the day and they parted on good terms to change for dinner.

As Lydia was checking her appearance in the mirror, a footman arrived with a hastily scribbled note from Alice. She read it with horror. Without a second thought she rushed to the door which led to Aubrey's domain and burst in. He was lounging on a chair with his feet on the fender, reading a newspaper.

'Aubrey, I have had the most dreadful news. You must help prevent the biggest scandal this county has ever seen.' She all but threw the letter into his hands and waited for his reaction.

'Dammit to hell! What is Lady Alice thinking? To elope with Duvall is the height of folly — I forgot to mention I had made enquiries about him and heard nothing to his credit. He might be the youngest son of an earl, but he is profligate and an inveterate gambler.'

Lydia was outraged at his comment. 'How could you be so stupid as to keep this information to yourself? If you had told me, then Alice would still be safe at home with her parents. She is in love with Duvall, but she is not stupid, and knowing he was a fortune-hunter could have prevented this disaster.' She wanted to pick up the nearest object and hurl it at it him.

He was on his feet, as angry as she. 'You are insolent, madam, and I suggest you hold your tongue.'

Perhaps she had been rather unwise to call him stupid, but Alice's elopement could have been prevented if he had bothered to pass on the crucial information he had obtained. She would not back down, and neither would she apologise. 'I had sought to ask for your help in this matter, but as your . . . your absent-mindedness is the main cause, I do not expect you to bother.'

If he had been a dragon he would be breathing fire — she could almost imagine smoke coming from his nostrils. His eyes were granite-hard, his lips thin and his stance rigid. She should have been terrified, ready to run away in case he decided to physically punish her for her temerity, but instead she was invigorated by the confrontation. Whatever she did, whatever she said, she knew he would never harm her.

She could almost hear his teeth grinding as he fought to control his temper. 'We must go after the girl. She has only just left, so I think I should be able to catch them up before they have travelled too far.' He frowned and paced the room for a moment. 'I shall ride ahead; you must follow in the carriage. Get your maid to pack an overnight bag for both of you and be ready to leave at once.'

'Do you think her parents have missed her? Will they not send out a search party themselves?'

'I expect the girl has told them she has a megrim and wishes to be left alone until the morning. Now, hurry up and get changed. We have not a moment to lose.'

Aubrey bundled her from the room and she could hear him shouting for his valet. Jenny was wringing her hands, distraught by her mistress's sudden disappearance. 'I must change into my travelling outfit, Jenny. You are to come with me, so make sure you pack a bag for yourself as well as me. I have never liked to be out in the dark, and I believe the weather could be turning colder as well.'

Her husband didn't come back to her, but a footman appeared to collect their bags and conduct them to the waiting coach. There were lanterns hanging on either side of the driver's box, and in their golden glow she saw flakes of snow falling.

Lydia was assisted into the carriage and was pleased to find hot bricks and furs ready inside to keep them warm. The carriage was pitch-black when the door was shut, as the blinds had been pulled down to keep their identities anonymous.

The coach rocked again alarmingly before the coachman snapped his whip and they rolled forward. 'I think His Grace must have arranged for extra men to accompany us, Jenny. At least four men climbed aboard just now, and if you listen carefully you can hear horses following behind, so we must have outriders as well.'

Lydia snuggled under the rugs and tried not to think what might happen if the duke did not catch up with Alice and her abductor. She could no longer think of Duvall as her friend's future husband, but as a villain hoping to marry an heiress in order to access her fortune for his own nefarious reasons. If Alice was obliged to spend a night in his company she would have no option but to marry him; Lydia prayed this would not be the case.

* * *

Aubrey kicked his stallion into a gallop. At least the ground was hard, as there had been no rain for a while. He hoped he had thought of everything; his valet had packed a bag with his essentials and had taken it down to the coach. He had two reliable, and discreet, men accompanying him and there were four armed men riding with Lydia.

He had decided the most likely direction for the runaway couple would be a toll road; these were well maintained and would allow Duvall's carriage to cover the distance more speedily than if they remained on the more obscure back roads. The note had been written at four o'clock; no doubt the girl had escaped soon after that, and therefore the two of them had been on the road for no more than an hour and a half. A rider travelled twice the speed as a coach, so with luck he would overtake them before any serious harm had been done to the girl's reputation.

Aubrey cursed himself for neglecting to pass on the information; Lydia had been right to blame him for this disaster. But whatever his failings, there would be a reckoning between them at some point. He would not be spoken to as if he were a badly behaved child; she must learn to curb her tongue and show him the respect he was due.

Thank God there was a full moon tonight, as it made his wild gallop that much safer. The wind rushed through his hair and he reached up and yanked his hat further down his forehead, then pulled up his muffler so only his eyes were visible.

Dammit! Now it was snowing. He hoped it would not turn into a blizzard. He had been travelling for just over an hour when he saw lights ahead: a coaching inn. Had the couple stopped here in the night, or were they going to push on and put as much distance between them and pursuit as they could? Aubrey smiled grimly. They did not know they were being pursued; they would think they had no need to hurry.

He brought his stallion to a rearing halt in the courtyard. His two men arrived minutes later and the three of them were dismounting when a brace of ostlers arrived. He addressed the least unsavoury. 'Has a carriage arrived in the past hour?'

The man tugged his forelock. 'It did, my lord, and they ain't gone nowhere neither. I reckon they've taken a room for the night. I'll get these beasts settled; you won't want to be riding no more tonight. We's in for a right old blizzard.'

'Jerry, Tom, arrange for accommodation and food as I told you, and then wait for me here.' He tossed them a handful of silver coins before striding into the dim interior of the inn. He almost brained himself on the beams and swore loudly.

'You have to be careful, my lord; them beams are a mite low for someone as tall as you. Are you wanting a room for the night?'

'I am looking for a young lady and gentleman — direct me to their chambers immediately.'

The landlord nodded and touched his nose. 'I thought there was something havey-cavey about them two. The gentleman is wetting his whistle in the bar, and the young lady is upstairs. I'll get the pot boy to take you.'

As Aubrey followed the lad through a maze of passageways, he was rehearsing what he could say to Lady Alice that would prevent her from having hysterics. He thanked God that Duvall was more interested in getting bosky than ravishing his future bride.

The boy indicated the door he needed and vanished. He knocked on the door and was asked to come in. 'Good evening, Lady Alice. I have come to take you home.' The girl was astonished by his sudden appearance. 'Sit down, child. There are things I must tell you and we might not have long before Duvall decides to investigate.' He waited until she was settled before continuing. She had yet to utter a sound and he hoped she would remain silent until he had finished. Instead of looking scandalised, or vehemently denying his accusations, she nodded sadly.

'Your Grace, I cannot tell you how glad I am to see you. We had not been travelling for more than a short distance before I realised the sort of man Captain Duvall actually was. He believed he had no more need to dissemble and I was in no position to refuse to marry him.'

'In which case, Lady Alice, we should be able to put matters straight. Tell me, did anybody see your face when you came in here?'

'No, Your Grace. I kept the hood of my cloak up.'

'Excellent news! Lydia is on her way here. As soon as she arrives you must exchange places. The landlord will think I am an irate husband chasing his errant wife. We shall stay here whilst you return. My carriage can take you back to Stenning, my staff are expecting you, and word will be sent to your parents that you are staying with us. Did you leave them a note as well?'

She nodded. 'Unfortunately, Your Grace, I told them I was running away to marry Captain Duvall and that by the time they read this letter it would be too late by then to intervene.'

'There is pen and paper on the desk; whilst we are waiting, write another note explaining you had a change of heart and came to stay with Lydia instead.'

He watched her scribble the missive. She folded it carefully. Aubrey pulled back the curtain and stared into the blackness. Thank God the snow appeared to have abated — his schemes would fail if the carriage became stuck. He calculated Lydia and her maid should arrive in another hour. That gave him sufficient time to deal with Duvall.

'Remain here and make sure you have packed everything. I'm going downstairs for a while.' She was doing her best not to cry and his heart went out to her. 'Don't worry, little one; you will come out of this unscathed. If Lydia and I insist that you have been with us all night then nobody will dare to question it.'

'I have been very silly, Your Grace. I am of a romantic nature, you know, and had quite set my heart on marrying a handsome cavalry officer. Lydia tried to warn me, but I had convinced myself I was in love with him.'

'Thank God you sent word to my wife. Now, sit quietly and don't worry. You will soon be on your way and no one will ever know what almost happened this evening.'

Remembering to duck his head, Aubrey found his way to the public bar. The sound of jollity and raised voices was enough to lead him there. He doubted Duvall would be wearing his uniform; he wouldn't want anyone to remember him. However, the bastard was easy to spot; he was propped against the bar, nursing a large tumbler of brandy as if he hadn't a care in the world.

Aubrey found the landlord and slipped him a silver coin. 'Make sure the gentleman believes his cattle are in need of his attention. I shall be waiting in the yard.'

Moments later Duvall staggered outside, muttering and cursing under his breath. 'Duvall, a word if you please,' Aubrey said to him.

Before the young man had time to react, a blanket had been thrown over his head and ropes secured around his shoulders and knees. 'Truss him up more soundly, men, and toss him in the back of his own carriage. I will deal with him tomorrow morning. When my coach arrives, have the horses changed and take the place of the coachman and groom. They will be half frozen by now.'

★   ★   ★

'I believe we are stopping, Your Grace. I think we must be at a coaching inn.'

'I'm not sure what His Grace has planned, Jenny, but I think we must remain inside until told otherwise.'

The men on the box scrambled down and they could hear the horses being changed again. This would be the second time the animals had been swapped; no doubt they would collect their own beasts on the return journey.

The door opened and her husband jumped in. 'Your maid must remain in here. You come with me, Lydia; I'm going to take you in the side door. Lady Alice will take your place and should be safe from harm before the night is out.' His voice was brusque. He had not forgiven her for her rudeness earlier.

Holding her cloak tight around her face, she followed him to a tiny sliver of light and then they were inside. Alice was waiting to embrace her. She was given no time to talk to her friend.

'Lady Alice, my man is waiting outside to escort you to the coach,' Aubrey said. 'Your bags are already stowed away. Travel safely and we will see you soon.' He all but pushed Alice through the door and then turned back to Lydia. 'We must wait here until the coach returns for us. The chamber is no more than adequate, but at least the linen is clean and there is a decent fire.' He gripped her elbow and led her up a narrow staircase and through a maze of passageways. He halted in front of a door. 'I must go outside for a while. I shall have a tray sent up for you. I shall see you in the morning.'

Leaving her to struggle with the latch, he strode off down the corridor. A loud thump, followed by language that made her blush, told her he had forgotten to duck and hit his head on the beam. It served him right for being so curmudgeonly — she smiled and, feeling considerably better, went into the chamber.

18

Aubrey rubbed his head and continued through the building and out through the side door. The two men who had travelled with Lydia were waiting for him; the coach had already departed. 'I shall come to the stables with you. There is something we have to do before we can retire.'

He explained his plan and they took him to the dilapidated, closed carriage in which Lady Alice had been transported and Duvall was now imprisoned. When they were within earshot the charade began.

'You must keep him quiet and secure in there until tomorrow,' Aubrey told the driver. 'I sent word to his commanding officer that he was a deserter before I set out. A message has now gone to the barracks with his locality. The army can deal with him now.'

'I reckon they'll hang him, Your Grace. They ain't too partial to their officers running away. Don't you worry; he's going nowhere.'

Aubrey nodded, satisfied Duvall would have heard every word and be desperate to escape. All that remained to do was for the men to carelessly leave the door open. With luck, that would be the last any of them heard of Duvall. Aubrey didn't want him returning to his mess and talking about what happened.

'Make sure he is able to breathe. I don't want a corpse on my hands in the morning.'

He left them to it and headed for the front entrance. He wished to speak to the landlord. Perhaps there was another room he could use, because it was going to be dammed difficult sharing a small chamber with Lydia and not be able to make love to her.

He had given her his word the marriage would remain unconsummated, but if she came to him he would

318

be unable to refuse. The more time he spent with her, the more he loved her. Although they were constantly at daggers drawn, he was convinced she no longer held him in dislike — but whether she had warmer feelings was unclear.

He hammered on the wooden table that served as a welcome desk. The landlord appeared, rubbing his hands on his grubby apron. 'Do you have a room for me, my man?'

'I don't; I'm that sorry, my lord. The lady took the last chamber.' He beamed and nodded his head vigourously, making the folds of his chin wobble. 'I can send up a fine supper for you both and plenty of hot water.'

'Very well. I shall find myself a drink before I go to my room. Do you have a private parlour available?'

'There's the Snug. I don't reckon it has more than a couple of gentlemen in there.'

'Have you got any spirits at this establishment?' The man nodded again.

'Then send whatever you have.' He called the man back. 'Send a supper tray to me; I shall eat in the Snug.'

He found himself a secluded corner, ignoring the other two occupants sitting in front of the fire. He devoured his meal, which was surprisingly tasty, and downed most of the bottle of brandy before he felt ready to go upstairs and join his wife.

★　★　★

Lydia occupied herself with unpacking her bag and shaking out the creases from tomorrow's gown. She placed her nightgown ready on a chair and waited in a fireside chair for the arrival of her supper tray. Hopefully, hot water would also arrive so that she could take a strip wash. There was a screen behind which was the commode and wash stand. Perfectly adequate for one night — her husband was going to find the accommodations at this inn rather primitive after Stenning Hall. How silly! He had been a soldier — he must have bivouacked in far worse places.

Someone knocked on the door and she hurried across to open it. Two boys staggered in, carrying giant jugs full of hot water. A girl followed with a tray from which appetising aromas wafted. She thanked them and gave them each a coin for their trouble.

Should she wash whilst the water was hot, or eat her supper? She decided on the latter and enjoyed the repast of vegetable soup, fresh bread and country cheese followed by large slice of fruit tart. She drank the porter with reluctance, but there was nothing else and she was thirsty.

She put the empty tray outside the door and then moved behind the screen. She stripped off her clothes and washed all over, feeling much better when she was completely clean and dry. As she was pulling on her nightgown she heard the door open. There had been no knock — was this Duvall come to find his bride?

She peered round the screen and watched as her husband pulled off his boots, removed his topcoat and cravat and flung himself full-length on the bed. His snores reverberated around the room in seconds. Feeling it safe to emerge, she crept over to stare at him in disgust. He was supposed to be sleeping elsewhere, and if he did have to share the room he should not have arrived in his cups and retired in his dirt. Her eyes watered at the stench of horse and unwashed male.

She could hardly climb into bed beside him even if she wished to. She wouldn't be able to sleep so close to that smell. Maybe if she shook his shoulder he would wake up and retire behind the screen for his ablutions. She attempted this but he remained comatose. The smell of brandy almost masked the other unpleasant odours.

She would have to make the best of it in the chair beside the fire, but the dratted man was on top of the covers so she would have to use her cloak to keep her warm. Heaven knew what he had done with his own caped riding coat.

She threw the remaining logs on the fire and prayed they would last until the morning. She was tempted to get dressed again; at least she would be warmer then. After two hours of listening to him enjoying his drunken slumber, she lost patience. Tossing her cloak to one side, she peeled back the comforter and squeezed into the small space he had left her. Then, bracing herself against the headboard, she placed her feet in the small of his back and heaved. For a moment he remained stationary, and then he began to move. She drew back her legs and kicked him as hard as she could. He shot off the edge and landed with a satisfactory thud on the boards.

Immediately she shook out the covers and took her rightful place inside. She was waiting for the explosion of wrath, but he remained silent. She snuggled down and prepared to go to sleep. He was an ex-soldier and could manage very well on the floor.

A slight groan from the far side of the bed indicated he was unharmed by her violent ejection. He was muttering and she pushed herself up in order to listen more carefully.

'What's that god-awful smell?' She heard him sniffing and then he coughed loudly. 'I stink like a midden. What the hell was I thinking of?' Further banging and shuffling followed then she hastily slid down and pulled the covers over her head as if she were sound asleep.

Perhaps he was too foxed to realise she was now occupying his place in the bed; she hadn't really thought this through. What was she going to do when he discovered her? From the noises on the far side of the room he had gone behind the screen and was washing. At least if they had to share the bed he would no longer smell like a stable hand.

Her pulse skittered. Where had that notion come from? Did she actually want him beside her with all that implied? She couldn't tell where he was. She opened her eyes and saw he was standing, entirely without garments, in front of the fire. He was drying his hair and the firelight outlined his form in the flickering gold. She was bewitched. She had never seen anything so beautiful; had never expected a naked male body would be of any interest. Her eyes moved along his wide, well-muscled shoulders, down his back and rested on his . . . She was hot all over and didn't understand what was happening to her.

To her horror he chose that moment to glance over his shoulder and caught her staring at him. 'I apologise for arriving in your chamber inebriated and stinking. I am now, as you can see, perfectly clean but I cannot promise I am not still slightly in my cups.' He seemed unbothered by his lack of clothes or her avid gaze. Casually he wrapped the large bath sheet around his hips and strolled across to sit beside her on the bed. 'Why do you braid your hair at night, darling? I don't like it — '

She had not been expecting him to criticise her appearance; was expecting some romantic nonsense, maybe even an apology for his nakedness. She sat up, which put her far too close to him, and tried to slide further back in the bed, but he followed her.

'Go away. I'm not comfortable with you sitting here. We are not properly dressed.'

'How observant you are, my love. I do so like that in a wife.' He smiled his devastating smile and her resistance crumbled.

She was not going to make it too easy for him — she would not give him the satisfaction of knowing that she loved him. Her eyes widened and hands flew to his chest. She spoke without thinking. 'I love you, Aubrey. I can't imagine how that has happened, for you are the most irritating man I've ever met.'

His expression changed, not to triumph at her capitulation, but to joy.

'I have loved you for years, darling girl, but only realised how I felt a few weeks ago.'

'I don't think I loved you then, my love. It has happened over the past few weeks. Mama said you had feelings for me but I didn't believe her. She will be so relieved this is indeed a love match.'

He reached out and drew her into his embrace. 'Are you sure you wish me to share your bed? I know I promised to keep my distance, but I love you so much all I can think about is making you my true wife.'

'There is only one bed, and I can hardly ask you to sleep on the floor, and I am certainly not going to. Therefore we must share, and I am not so naive as to think that a naked man invited to my bed will wish to spend the night in slumber.'

He pulled back the covers and grasped the hem of her nightgown. To her astonishment, instead of asking her to raise her bottom so he could take it off, he ripped it in half, leaving her in the same state as him.

'Now, I shall unbind your hair; and then, my darling, I shall show you how much I truly love you.'

THE END

Other titles in the
Linford Romance Library:

MORE THAN A PORTRAIT

Diana Dennison

When Jane is offered a job in northern Italy, with its promise of sunshine and colour, mountains and romantic scenery, her adventurous spirit can hardly refuse. Then she meets her employer: the unpredictable, pompous and dictatorial Duncan Frobisher. Sparks immediately fly between them, and Jane comes to know more than her fair share of elation and black depression before her temporary employment comes to an end . . .